The Seducer's Diary

SØREN KIERKEGAARD

The Seducer's Diary

Edited by VICTOR EREMITA
Translated by ALASTAIR HANNAY

GREAT  LOVES

4 99

PENGUIN BOOKS

Published by the Penguin Group
Penguin Books Ltd, 80 Strand, London WC2R ORL, England
Penguin Group (USA) Inc., 375 Hudson Street, New York, New York 10014, USA
Penguin Group (Canada), 90 Eglinton Avenue East, Suite 700, Toronto, Ontario, Canada M4P 2Y3
(a division of Pearson Penguin Canada Inc.)
Penguin Ireland, 25 St Stephen's Green, Dublin 2, Ireland
(a division of Penguin Books Ltd)
Penguin Group (Australia), 250 Camberwell Road, Camberwell, Victoria 3124, Australia
(a division of Pearson Australia Group Pty Ltd)
Penguin Books India Pvt Ltd, 11 Community Centre, Panchsheel Park, New Delhi – 110 017, India
Penguin Group (NZ), 67 Apollo Drive, Rosedale, North Shore 0632, New Zealand
(a division of Pearson New Zealand Ltd)
Penguin Books (South Africa) (Pty) Ltd, 24 Sturdee Avenue,
Rosebank, Johannesburg 2196, South Africa

Penguin Books Ltd, Registered Offices: 80 Strand, London WC2R ORL, England

www.penguin.com

This translation first published in Penguin Books 1992
This edition published in Penguin Books 2007

2

Translation copyright © Alastair Hannay, 1992
All rights reserved

The moral right of the translator has been asserted

Set in 9/11 pt Adobe Caslon
Typeset by Rowland Phototypesetting Ltd, Bury St Edmunds, Suffolk
Printed in England by Clays Ltd, St Ives plc

978-0-141-03281-8

This edition produced for The Book People Ltd,
Hall Wood Avenue, Haydock, St Helens WA11 9UL

Søren Aabye Kierkegaard (1813–1855) was a nineteenth-century Danish philosopher and theologian, generally recognized as the first existentialist philosopher. Kierkegaard's childhood was an isolated and unhappy one, clouded by the religious fervour of his father. Towards the end of his university career, he started to criticize the Christianity upheld by his father and to look for a new set of values. In 1841 he broke off his engagement to Regine Olsen and devoted himself to writing. During the next ten years he produced a flood of discourses and no fewer than twelve major philosophical essays, many of them written under *noms de plume*. *Either/Or*, from which *The Seducer's Diary* is taken, is the earliest of his major works. A masterpiece of duality, *Either/Or* is an exploration of the conflict between the aesthetic and the ethical.

Sua passion' predominante
È la giovin principiànte.
              Don Giovanni, Act I

I cannot conceal from myself, can scarcely master, the anxiety which grips me at this moment, as I resolve for my own interest to make a fair copy of the hasty transcript I was able at that time to secure only in the greatest haste and with much disquiet. The situation confronts me just as alarmingly, but also just as reproachfully, as it did then. Contrary to his custom, he had not closed his escritoire, so its whole contents lay at my disposal; but it is futile for me to gloss over my behaviour by reminding myself that I did not open any drawer. One drawer was pulled out. In it I found a pile of loose papers and on top of them lay a book in broad quarto, tastefully bound. On the side facing up was a vignette of white paper on which he had written in his own hand 'Commentarius perpetuus No. 4'. In vain have I tried, however, to make myself believe that had that side of the book not been turned up, and had the strange title not tempted me, I should not have succumbed to the temptation, or at least would have attempted to resist it. The title itself was curious, not so much in itself as because of its setting. From a quick glance at the loose papers I saw that these contained constructions of erotic situations, some hints about some relationship or other, sketches of letters of a quite peculiar character, with which I later became familiar in their artistically consummate, calculated carelessness. When now, having seen through the designing mind of this depraved person, I recall my situation; when, with an eye open for every artifice, I approach that drawer in thought, it makes the same impression upon me as it must make upon a police officer when he enters the room of a forger, opens his repositories and finds in a drawer a pile of loose papers, handwriting samples; on one there is part of a foliage motif, on another a signature, on a third a line of reversed writing. It shows him clearly that he is on the right track, and his joy over this is mingled with a certain admiration for the study and industry here clearly in evidence.

For me it might have been a little different, being less used to tracking down criminals and not armed with, well, a police badge. The fact that I was following unlawful paths would have been an additional weight on my mind. On this occasion, as usually happens, I was no less at a loss for thoughts than for words. An impression remains with one until reflection reasserts itself and, diverse and speedy in its movements, ingratiates itself with the unfamiliar stranger and talks him round. The more reflection develops, the quicker it can pull itself together; like a passport clerk for foreign travellers, it becomes so used to seeing the most fantastic figures that it is not easily taken aback. But however strongly developed my own reflection, I was at first still greatly astonished. I remember very well that I turned pale, that I nearly fell over, and how that fact alarmed me. What if he had come home, had found me in a faint with the drawer in my hand? At least a bad conscience can make life interesting.

The title of the book in itself made no particular impression on me; I thought it was a collection of excerpts, which to me seemed quite natural since I knew that he had always embraced his studies with enthusiasm. Its contents, however, were of quite another kind. It was neither more nor less than a diary, painstakingly kept; and just as I did not think, from what I knew of him before, that his life was in such great need of commentary, so I do not deny, after the insight I had now gained, that the title had been chosen with much taste and understanding, with true aesthetic, objective mastery of himself and the situation. The title is in perfect harmony with the entire contents. His life has been an attempt to realize the task of living poetically. With a keenly developed sense for what is interesting in life, he had known how to find it, and having found it he had constantly reproduced the experience in a semi-poetic way. His diary, therefore, was not historically exact or a straightforward narrative, not indicative, but subjunctive. Although of course the experience was recorded after it happened – sometimes perhaps even a considerable time after – it was often described as if taking place at the very moment, so dramatically vivid that sometimes it was as though it was all taking place before one's very eyes. But that he should have done this because the diary served any ulterior purpose is highly improbable; it is quite obvious that, in the strictest sense, its only importance was for him personally. And to assume that what I have before me is a literary work, perhaps even intended for publication, is precluded by the whole as well as by the details. Certainly he did not need to fear anything personally in publishing it, for most of the names are so unusual that there is altogether no likelihood of their being authentic. But I have formed a suspicion that the Christian name is historically correct, so that he himself would always be sure of identifying the actual person, while every outsider must be misled by the surname. Such at least is the case with the girl I knew, around whom the chief interest centres, Cordelia – that was her correct name; not, however, Wahl.

How, then, can we explain that the diary has nevertheless acquired such a poetic flavour? The answer is not difficult; it can be explained by his poetic temperament, which is, if you will, not rich, or if you prefer, not poor enough to distinguish poetry and reality from each other. The poetic was the extra he himself brought with him. This extra was the poetical element he enjoyed in the poetic situation provided by reality; this element he took back in again in the form of poetic reflection. That was the second enjoyment, and enjoyment was what his whole life was organized around. In the first case he savoured the aesthetic element personally; in the second he savoured his own person aesthetically. In the first case the point was that he egoistically, personally, savoured what in part reality gave him and what in part he himself had impregnated reality with; in the second case his personality was volatilized and he savoured, then, the situation and himself in the situation. In the first case he was in constant need of reality as the occasion, as an element; in the second case reality was drowned in the poetic. The fruit of the first stage is thus the mood from which the diary results as the fruit of the second stage, the word 'fruit' being used in the latter case in a somewhat different sense from that in the first. The poetic is thus something he has constantly possessed by virtue of the ambiguity in which his life passed.

Behind the world we live in, in the distant background, lies another world standing in roughly the same relation to the former as the stage one sometimes sees in the theatre behind the real stage stands to the latter. Through a thin gauze one sees what looks like a world of gossamer, lighter, more ethereal, of a different quality from the real world. Many people who appear bodily in the real world do not belong there but to this other world. Yet the fact that someone fades away in this manner, indeed almost disappears from reality, can be due to either health or sickness. The latter was the case with this person, with whom I was once acquainted but without getting to know him. He did not belong to reality yet had much to do with it. He was constantly running around in it, yet even when he devoted himself to it most, he was already beyond it. But it was not the good that beckoned him away, nor was it really evil – even now I dare not say that of him. He has suffered from an *exacerbatio cerebri* for which reality afforded insufficient incitement, at best only temporarily. Reality was not too much for him, he was not too weak to bear its burden; no, he was too strong, but this strength was a sickness. As soon as reality lost its power to incite he was disarmed; that is where the evil in him lay. He was conscious of this, even at the moment of incitement, and it was in his consciousness of this the evil lay.

I once knew the girl whose story forms the substance of the diary. Whether he has seduced others I do not know; it does seem so from his papers. He seems also to have been adept at another kind of practice, wholly characteristic of him; for he was of far too spiritual a nature to be a seducer in the usual sense. From the diary we also learn that at times his desire was for something altogether arbitrary – a greeting, for instance – and under no circumstance would accept more, because in the person in question this was what was most beautiful. With the help of his mental gifts he knew how to tempt a girl, to draw her to him, without caring to possess her in any stricter sense. I can imagine him able to bring a girl to the point where he was sure she would sacrifice all, but when matters had come that far he left off without the slightest advance having been made on his part, and without a word having been let fall of love, let alone a declaration, a promise. Yet it would have happened, and the unhappy girl would retain the consciousness of it with double bitterness, because there was not the slightest thing she could appeal to. She could only be constantly tossed about by the most divergent moods in a terrible witches' dance, at one moment reproaching herself, forgiving him, at another reproaching him, and then, since the relationship would only have been actual in a figurative sense, she would constantly have to contend with the doubt that the whole thing might only have been imagination. She would be unable to confide in anyone, for really there was nothing to confide. When you have dreamed, you can tell others your dream, but what she had to tell was no dream, it was reality, and yet, as soon as she wanted to speak of it to another to ease her troubled mind, it was nothing. She herself felt this very keenly. No one could grasp it, hardly even herself, and yet it lay with an unsettling weight upon her.

Such victims were therefore of a quite special nature. They were not unfortunate girls who, social outcasts or thinking themselves such, openly fumed and fretted and now and then, when their hearts became too full, gave vent in hate or forgiveness. No visible change occurred in them; they lived in their normal circumstances, as respected as ever, and yet they were changed, well-nigh inexplicably to themselves, incomprehensibly to others. Their lives were not, as with those others, snapped off or broken, they were bent in on themselves; lost to others, they sought vainly to find themselves. Just as you might say that your path through life left no trace (for your feet were so formed as to leave no footprints – this is how I best picture to myself his infinite self-reflection), so it could be said that no victim fell to him. He lived in far too spiritual a manner to be a seducer in the ordinary sense. Sometimes, however, he assumed a parastatic body and was then sheer sensuality. Even his affair with Cordelia was so complicated that it was possible for him to appear as the one seduced; yes, even the unlucky girl was sometimes in confusion about it; here, too, his footprints are so indistinct that any proof is impossible. The individuals were merely his incitement; he cast them off as a tree sheds its leaves – he is refreshed, the leaf withers.

But how, I wonder, do things look in his own head? Just as he has led others astray, so in my view he ends by going astray himself. It is not in external respects that he has led the others astray, but in ways that affect them inwardly. There is something outrageous in a person's misdirecting a traveller who has lost his way and then leaving him to himself in his error, yet what is that compared with causing someone to go astray in himself? The lost traveller, after all, has a consolation that the country around him is constantly changing, and with every change is born a new hope of finding a way out. A person who goes astray inwardly has less room for manoeuvre; he soon finds he is going round in a circle from which he cannot escape. This, on an even more terrible scale, I think, is how it will go with him. I can imagine nothing more agonizing than an intriguing mind which has lost the thread and then turns all its wits upon itself, as conscience awakens and the question is one of extricating oneself from this confusion. It is to no avail that he has many exits from his fox's earth; the moment his anxious soul thinks it sees daylight appearing, it proves to be a new entrance, and like startled game, pursued by despair, he is thus constantly seeking an exit and forever finding an entrance through which he returns into himself. Such a man is not always what we could call a criminal; often he himself is deluded by his intrigues, and yet he is overtaken by a more terrible punishment than the criminal, for what is the pain even of remorse compared with this conscious madness? His punishment has a purely aesthetic character, for even to talk of his conscience awakening is to apply too ethical an expression to him. For him conscience takes the form simply of a higher level of consciousness which expresses itself in a disquietude that still fails to accuse him in a deeper sense, but which keeps him awake with no support beneath him in his barren restlessness. Nor is he mad; for in their diversity his finite thoughts are not petrified in the eternity of madness.

Poor Cordelia! For her, too, it will be hard to find peace. She forgives him from the bottom of her heart, but she finds no rest, for then doubt awakens: it was she who broke off the engagement, it was she who caused the disaster, it was her pride that yearned for the uncommon. Then she repents, but she finds no rest, for then the accusing thoughts acquit her: it was he with his artfulness who placed this plan in her mind. Then she turns to hatred, her heart finds relief in curses, but she finds no rest; she reproaches herself again, reproaches herself because she has hated, she who is herself a sinner, reproaches herself because, however sly he may have been, she will still always be guilty. It is grievous for her that he has deceived her; it is even more grievous, one could almost be tempted to say, that he has aroused in her this many-tongued reflection, that he has developed her aesthetically enough no longer to listen humbly to one voice, but to be able to hear these many points of view all at once. Then memory awakens with her soul, she forgets the offence and the guilt, she remembers the beautiful moments, and she is numbed in an unnatural exaltation. In such moments she not only remembers him, she understands him with a clairvoyance which only goes to show how far she has travelled. Then she no longer sees the criminal in him, or the noble person; her sense of him is purely aesthetic. She once wrote me a note in which she expressed her feelings about him. 'Sometimes he was so spiritual that I felt myself annihilated as a woman, at other times so wild and passionate, so filled with desire, that I almost trembled before him. Sometimes I seemed a stranger to him, at other times he gave of himself completely; when I then flung my arms around him, sometimes everything was suddenly changed and I embraced a cloud. I knew that expression before I knew him, but he has taught me what it means; when I use it I always think of him, just as every thought I think is only in connection with him. I have always loved music and he was a matchless instrument; always alive, he had a range that no instrument has, he was the epitome of all feelings and moods, no thought was too elevated for him, none too despairing, he could roar like an autumn storm, he could whisper inaudibly. No word of mine was without effect, and yet I cannot say that my word did not fail of its effect, for it was impossible for me to know what effect it would have. With an indescribable but secret, blessed, unnameable anxiety I listened to this music I myself called forth, yet did not call forth; there was always harmony, he always carried me away.'

Terrible for her, it will be more terrible for him; I can infer this from the fact that even I cannot quite control the anxiety that grips me every time I think of the matter. I, too, am carried along into that nebulous realm, that dream world where every moment one is afraid of one's own shadow. Often I try in vain to tear myself away, I follow as a figure of menace, as an accuser who cannot speak. How strange! He has spread the deepest secrecy over everything, and still there is a deeper secret, and it is this, that I am in on it; and indeed I have myself become privy to it unlawfully. To forget the whole thing would be impossible. I have sometimes thought of speaking about it to him. Still, how would that help? He would disavow everything, maintain that the diary was a literary effort, or impose silence upon me, something I could not deny him considering how I came to know of it. Nothing, after all, is so pervaded by seduction and damnation as a secret.

I have received from Cordelia a collection of letters. Whether these are all of them I do not know, although it occurs to me she once let it be understood that she herself had confiscated some. I have copied them and will now insert them in my own clean copy. It is true the dates are missing, but even if they were there it would not help much, since the diary as it proceeds becomes more and more sparing. Indeed, in the end, with the odd exception, it gives no dates, as though the story as it progressed acquired such qualitative importance, and in spite of being historically real, came so near to being idea, that time specifications became for this reason a matter of indifference. What did help me, however, was the fact that at various places in the diary are some words whose significance at first I did not grasp. But by comparing them with the letters I realized that they furnish the motives for the latter. It will therefore be a simple matter to insert them in the right places, inasmuch as I shall always introduce the letter at the point where its motive is indicated. Had I not found these clues, I would have incurred a misunderstanding; for no doubt it would not have occurred to me, as now from the diary seems probable, that at times the letters followed upon each other with such frequency that she seems to have received several in one day. Had I followed my original intention I should have apportioned them more evenly, and not suspected the effect he obtained through the passionate energy with which he used this, like all other means, to keep Cordelia on the pinnacle of passion.

Apart from complete information on his relationship to Cordelia, the diary also contained, interspersed here and there, several small descriptions. Wherever these were found there was an 'NB' in the margin. These depictions have absolutely nothing to do with Cordelia's story but have given me a vivid conception of what is meant by an expression he often used, though previously I understood it differently: 'One ought always to have an extra little line out.' Had an earlier volume of this diary fallen into my hands, I should probably have come across more of these, which somewhere in the margin he calls 'actions at a distance'; for he himself admits that Cordelia occupied him too much for him really to have time to look about.

Shortly after he had abandoned Cordelia, he received some letters from her which he returned unopened. These were among the letters Cordelia turned over to me. She had herself broken the seal, and so there seems no reason why I should not venture to make a transcript. She has never mentioned their content to me; on the other hand, when she referred to her relationship to Johannes she usually recited a little verse, I believe by Goethe, which seemed to convey a different meaning according to her moods and the difference in delivery these occasioned:

> *Gehe*
> *Verschmähe*
> *Die Treue,*
> *Die Reue*
> *Kommt nach.*

These letters go as follows:

Johannes!

I do not call you 'mine', I realize very well you never have been, and I am punished enough by this thought having once gladdened my soul; and yet I do call you 'mine': my seducer, my deceiver, my foe, my murderer, source of my unhappiness, grave of my joy, abyss of my ruin. I call you 'mine', and call myself 'yours'; and as it once flattered your ear, which proudly bent down to my adoration, so shall it now sound like a curse upon you, a curse to all eternity. Don't expect me to pursue you, or to arm myself with a dagger so as to incite your ridicule! Flee where you will, I am still yours; go to the farthest boundaries of the world, I am still yours; love a hundred others, I am still yours; yes, even in the hour of death I am yours. The very language I use against you must prove I am yours. You have presumed so to deceive a human being that you have become everything to me; so now will I place all my pleasure in being your slave – yours, yours, yours is what I am, your curse.

Your Cordelia

Johannes!

There was a rich man who had many cattle, large and small; there was a poor little girl, she had only a single lamb, which ate from her hand and drank from her cup. You were the rich man, rich in all the earth's splendour, I was the poor girl who owned only my love. You took it, you rejoiced in it; then desire beckoned to you and you sacrificed the little I owned; of your own you could sacrifice nothing. There was a rich man who owned many cattle, large and small; there was a poor little girl who had only her love.

Your Cordelia

Johannes!

Is there no hope at all, then? Will your love never reawaken?

I know you have loved me, even if I do not know what makes me sure of that. I will wait, however heavy time hangs, I will wait, wait until you are weary of loving others; your love will then rise up again from its grave, I will love you as always, thank you as always, as before, oh Johannes, as before! Johannes! This cold-hearted callousness against me, is it your true nature? Was your love, your ample heart just a lie and a falsehood? Are you now yourself again, then? Be patient with my love, forgive me for continuing to love you; I know my love is a burden to you, but there will be a time when you return to your Cordelia. Your Cordelia! Hear that entreaty! Your Cordelia, your Cordelia.

Your Cordelia

If Cordelia did not possess the compass she admired in her Johannes, one still sees clearly that she was not without modal variation. Each of her letters clearly bears the stamp of her mood, even though to some extent she lacked lucidity in her presentation. This is especially the case in the second letter, where one suspects rather than grasps her meaning, but to me it is this imperfection that makes it so touching.

April 4th

Caution, my beautiful unknown! Caution! Stepping out of a coach is not so simple a matter. Sometimes it is a decisive step. I might lend you a short story by Tieck in which you would see how a lady, on dismounting from her horse, got so caught up in a tangle that this step became decisive for her whole life. Also, the steps on coaches are usually so badly placed that one has almost to forget about being graceful and risk a desperate lunge into the arms of coachman and footman. Yes, coachman and footman have the best of it! I really think I shall seek employment as a footman in a house where there are young girls; a servant easily becomes privy to the secrets of a little girl like that. But for God's sake, don't jump, I beg you! After all, it's dark; I shan't disturb you; I shall just place myself under this street-lamp so you can't see me, and one is always only bashful, after all, to the extent one is seen, but then again, one is always only seen to the extent one sees. So for the sake of the footman who may not be able to withstand such a leap, for the sake of the silk dress, likewise the lace edging, for my sake, let this charming little foot, whose slenderness I have already admired, let it venture out into the world, dare to depend on it, it will surely find a footing, and should you tremble an instant because it seems as though it sought in vain for something to rest upon, yes, should you tremble even after it has found it, then quickly bring the other foot too, for who would be so cruel as to leave you in that position, who so ungracious, so slow to keep up with the revelation of beauty? Or is it, again, some intruder you fear? Hardly the servant, or me, for I have already seen the little foot, and since I am a natural scientist I have learned from Cuvier how to draw definite conclusions from such details. Hurry then! How this anxiety enhances your beauty! Still, anxiety in itself is not beautiful; it is so only when one sees at the same time the energy that overcomes it. How firmly, now, this little foot stands. I have noticed that girls with small feet generally stand more firmly than the more pedestrian, large-footed ones. – Now who would have thought it? It flies in the face of all experience, one runs not nearly so great a risk of one's dress being caught up when climbing out as when one jumps out. But then it is always risky for young girls to ride in a coach, in the end they come to stay there. The lace and the ribbons are lost and that's the end of that. No one has seen anything; to be sure a dark figure appears, wrapped to the eyes in a cloak. One cannot see where he has come from, the light shines right in one's eyes; he passes you by in a moment, when you are about to enter the street-door. Just at the critical second, a sidelong glance seizes upon its object. You blush, your bosom becomes too full to be able to lighten itself in a single breath; there is exasperation in your glance, a proud contempt; there is a prayer, a tear in your eye; both are equally beautiful, I accept both equally as my due, for I can be just as well the one thing as the other. But I'm mischievous all the same – what is the number of the house? What do I see? A window-display of trinkets; my beautiful unknown, perhaps it is outrageous of me, but I follow the path of light ... She has forgotten what has passed. Ah, yes, when one is seventeen, when one goes shopping at that happy age, when the thought of every large or small object one lays one's hand on gives an inexpressible joy, one forgets easily. She still hasn't seen me. I am standing by myself, far away on the other side of the counter. A mirror hangs on the wall opposite. She doesn't think of it, but it thinks of her. How true to her image it is, as a humble slave who shows his devotion by being faithful, a slave who, although she means something to him, means nothing to her, who although he dares to grasp her, does not dare to comprehend her. That unhappy mirror, which can capture her image but not her; that unhappy mirror, which cannot hide her image in its secret depths, hide it from the whole world, but must on the contrary betray it to others, as now to me. What agony if a man were so made. And yet aren't there many who are made thus, who own nothing except in the instant when they show it to others, who grasp the surface only, not the substance, who lose everything when the substance itself wants to appear, as this mirror would lose her image if she were, with a single breath, to betray her heart to it? And if a man could not possess a memory image even at the moment of presence, he would always want to be at a distance from the beauty, not too near for the earthly eye to see how beautiful is that which he holds in his close embrace and is lost to the outward eye, though he can always regain it by putting it at a distance, but which he can then also have before him in his mind's eye when he cannot see the object itself because it is too near, when lips are closed on lips ... Yet, how beautiful she is! Poor mirror, it must be agony! It is well that you know no jealousy. Her head is a perfect oval; she inclines it a little forward, thus heightening her forehead, which rises pure and proud without any phrenologist's signs of intellect. Her dark hair closes softly and gently about her brow. Her face is like a fruit, every transition fully rounded. Her skin is transparent, like velvet to the touch, I can feel it with my eyes. Her eyes – well, yes, I haven't seen them yet, they are hidden behind lids armed with silken fringes curving like hooks, dangerous to whoever would meet her glance. She has a Madonna head, pure and innocent in cast; and like the Madonna she is bending forward, but she is not lost in contemplation of the One. There is a variation of expression in her face. What she is considering is the manifold, the multiplicity of things over which worldly pomp and splendour casts its reflection. She pulls off her glove to show the mirror and myself a right hand, white and shapely as an antique, without adornment, not even a flat gold ring on her fourth finger – Bravo! She looks up, and how changed everything is, yet the same, the forehead a little less high, the oval of her face a little less regular but more alive. She is talking with the salesman, she is cheerful, joyful, talkative. She has already chosen one, two, three things; she picks up a fourth and holds it in her hand, again she looks down; she asks what it costs; she puts it to one side under her glove, it must surely be a secret, intended for – a sweetheart? But then she is not engaged. Alas, there are many who are not engaged and yet have a sweetheart, many who are engaged and still have no sweetheart ... Ought I to give her up? Ought I to leave her undisturbed in her joy? ... She wants to pay, but she has lost her purse ... presumably she mentions her address, I don't want to hear that, I don't want to deprive myself of the surprise; I shall no doubt meet her again in life, I shall recognize her, and maybe she will also recognize me, my sidelong glance is not so easily forgotten. When I meet her by surprise in unexpected surroundings, that's when her turn will come. If she does not recognize me, if her glance does not immediately convince me of that, then I can always get a chance to see her from the side. I promise she shall remember the situation. No impatience, no greediness, everything will be savoured in slow draughts; she is earmarked and she will no doubt be brought in.

the 5th

I rather like that! Alone in the evening on Østergade. Yes, all right, I can see the footman following you; don't suppose I think so ill of you that you would go out all alone; don't think I am so inexperienced that in my survey of the situation I have not observed that demure figure straightaway. But why in such a hurry? One is a little anxious after all; one feels a pounding of the heart, due not to an impatient longing to get home, but to an impatient fear which courses through one's entire body with its sweet unrest, and hence the rapid tempo of the feet. – But still it is gorgeous, priceless to walk alone like this – with the footman behind . . . 'One is sixteen years old, one has read, that is to say, read romances. While happening to pass through one's brothers' room one has picked up a piece of a conversation between them and their friends, something about Østergade. Later one has whisked through on several occasions to obtain a little more information if possible. To no avail! As a big, grown-up girl, shouldn't one know something about the world? If only it were possible to go out without the servant behind. Thanks, no! Mother and father would make peculiar faces, and also, what excuse could one give? There's no chance of it when one is going to a party, it would be a little too early; I heard August say nine to ten o'clock. Going home it's too late, and then usually you must have an escort to drag along. Thursday evening, on the way back from the theatre, would be a splendid opportunity, but then one always has to drive in the coach and have Mrs Thomsen and her dear cousins packed in too; if one drove alone, one could let down the window and look about a bit. Still, the unexpected often occurs. Today mother said to me, "You'll never get that sewing finished for your father's birthday; to be quite undisturbed, you may go to your Aunt Jette's and stay until tea-time, then Jens can fetch you!" Really it wasn't such a very pleasing message, since it is extremely boring at Aunt Jette's; but then I will walk home alone at nine with the servant. When Jens comes, he will have to wait until a quarter to ten, and then off we go. Only I may meet my Mr Broder or Mr August – that mightn't be such a good idea, presumably I'd be escorted home – thanks, but I prefer to be free, freedom – but if I could catch sight of them so that they didn't see me' . . . Now then, my little lady, what is it you see, and what do you think I see? In the first place, the little cap you have on suits you splendidly, and harmonizes totally with your hurrying. It is not a hat, nor is it a bonnet, more like a kind of hood. But you can't possibly have had that on when you went out this morning. Could the servant have brought it, or have you borrowed it from Aunt Jette? – Maybe you are incognito. One shouldn't lower the veil completely if one is to make observations. Or perhaps it isn't a veil but just a broad piece of lace? In the dark it is impossible to decide. Whatever it is, it hides the upper part of the face. The chin is really pretty, a little too pointed; the mouth small, open; that's because you are walking too energetically. The teeth – white as snow. That's how it should be. Teeth are of the greatest importance, they are a lifeguard hiding behind the seductive softness of the lips. The cheeks glow with health. – If one inclines one's head a little to the side it might be possible to catch a glimpse under the veil or lace. Watch out! A look like that from below is more dangerous than one from straight ahead. It's like fencing, and what weapon so sharp, so sudden in its movement, and hence so deceptive, as the eye? One points high quart, as the fencer says, and thrusts in second; the quicker the thrust follows the pointing the better. The moment of targetting is an indescribable now. The opponent feels as though slashed, yes, indeed he is struck, but in quite a different place than he thought . . . indefatigably, on she goes without fear and without harm. Watch out! There's a man coming over there; lower the veil, don't let his profane glance defile you. You've no idea – it might be impossible for you to forget for a long time the disgusting dread with which it touched you. – You do not notice, as I did, that he has sized up the situation. – The servant has been picked out as the nearest object. Yes, now you see the consequences of going out alone with a servant. The servant has fallen down. Really, it's quite laughable, but what will you do now? Going back and helping him to his feet is impossible, to go on with a mud-stained servant is disagreeable, to go alone is risky. Watch out! the monster approaches . . . You don't answer me. Just look at me, is there anything in my appearance that frightens you? I make no impression at all on you, I look like a good-natured person from quite another world. There is nothing in my speech to disturb you, nothing to remind you of the situation, no slightest movement of mine that comes too near you. You are still a little anxious; you still haven't forgotten that sinister figure's approach. You conceive a certain kindness towards me, the awkwardness that keeps me from looking at you gives you the upper hand. That pleases you and makes you feel safe. You might almost be tempted to poke a little fun at me. I wager that at this moment you would have the courage to take me by the arm, if it occurred to you . . . So it's in Stormgade you live. You drop me a cold and hasty curtsy. Have I deserved that, I who have helped you out of the whole unpleasantness? You are sorry, you return, you thank me for my civility, offer me your hand – why do you turn pale? Isn't my voice unchanged, my bearing the same, my eye as quiet and calm? This handclasp? Can a handclasp mean anything? Yes, much, very much, my little miss. Within a fortnight I shall explain everything to you; until then you must remain in the contradiction: I am a good-natured person who came like a knight to the aid of a young girl, and I can also press your hand in a way that is anything but good-natured. –

April 7th

'On Monday, then, one o'clock at the exhibition.' Very good, I shall have the honour of turning up at a quarter to one. A little rendezvous. Last Saturday I finally cut the matter short and decided to call on my much-travelled friend, Adolph Bruun. To that end I set out at about seven in the evening for Vestergade, where someone had told me he was living. However, he was not there, not even on the third floor, which I reached quite out of breath. As I was about to descend, my ear caught the sound of a melodious feminine voice saying, 'On Monday, then, one o'clock at the exhibition; the others are all out then, but you know I never dare see you at home.' The invitation was not to me but to a young man who was out of the door in a flash, and so quickly that not even my eye, let alone my legs, could catch him. Why is there no gaslight on the stairway? At least I might have seen whether it was worthwhile being so punctual. Still, if there had been a gaslight I might not have heard. What exists is the rational, after all; I am and remain an optimist . . . Now, which one is her? The exhibition is swarming with girls, to quote Donna Anna. It is exactly a quarter to one. My beautiful unknown! Would that your intended were in every way as punctual as I; or perhaps you would rather he never came a quarter of an hour too early; as you will, I am in every way at your service . . . Bewitching enchantress, witch or fairy, let your cloud vanish, reveal yourself, you are presumably already here, but invisible to me; betray yourself, for I hardly dare expect any other kind of revelation. Could there perhaps be several up here on the same errand as she? Quite possibly. Who knows the ways of man, even when he goes to exhibitions? – But there comes a young girl in the front room, hurrying, faster than a bad conscience after a sinner. She forgets to hand over her ticket and the man in red stops her. Heaven preserve us! What a rush she's in! It must be her. Why such premature impetuosity? It still isn't one o'clock. Do but remember that you are to meet the beloved. Is it no matter at all how one looks on such occasions, or is this what it means to put one's best foot forward? When such an innocent young hot-head keeps a tryst, she tackles the matter like a madwoman. She is all of a flutter. As for me, I sit here comfortably in my chair, contemplating a delightful pastoral landscape . . . She's a devil's child, she storms through all the rooms. You must learn to hide your eagerness a little; remember for example what was said to Lisbeth: 'Does it become a young girl to let it be seen how eager she is to pair?' But of course your meeting is one of those innocent ones . . . Lovers usually consider a tryst a most beautiful moment. I myself still remember as clearly as if it were yesterday the first time I hastened to the appointed place, with a heart as full as it was ignorant of the joy awaiting me, the first time I knocked three times, the first time the window was opened, the first time the little door was opened by the invisible hand of a girl who concealed herself in opening it, the first time I hid a girl under my cloak in the light summer night. But much illusion is blended with this judgement. The dispassionate third party does not always find the lovers most beautiful at this moment. I have been witness to trysts where, although the girl was charming and the man handsome, the whole impression was well-nigh disgusting and the meeting itself far from beautiful, though no doubt it seemed so to the lovers. In a way one gains something by becoming more experienced; for although one loses the sweet unrest of impatient longing, one gains a preparedness to make the moment really beautiful. It can irritate me to see a man given such an opportunity so bewildered that love alone is enough to give him delirium tremens. But what does the farmer know of cucumber salad? Instead of being level-headed enough to enjoy her disquiet, to allow it to enflame her beauty and kindle it, he produces only a charmless confusion, and yet he goes joyfully home imagining it to have been something glorious . . . But what the devil has become of the fellow? It's already two o'clock. What fine types, these sweethearts! A scoundrel like that lets a young girl wait for him! Not me, I'm a trustworthy person of quite different calibre! Maybe it would be best to speak to her now, since she is passing by for the fifth time. 'Pardon my boldness, fair young lady. You are no doubt looking for your family up here. You have hurried past me several times, and as my eyes followed you, I noticed you always stop in the next but last room; perhaps you are unaware that there is still another room further in. Perhaps you will find them there.' She curtsies to me; it suits her well. The occasion is favourable. I am glad the person has not come; one always fishes best in troubled waters. When a young girl is emotionally disturbed, one can successfully venture that which would otherwise be ill-starred. I have just bowed to her as politely and distantly as possible. I sit down again in my chair, look at my landscape, and watch her. To follow her straightaway would be too risky; she might find me intrusive and then immediately be on her guard. Just now she believes I addressed her out of sympathy, I am in her good books. – I know quite well there's not a soul in the inner room. Solitude will have a beneficial effect upon her. So long as she sees many people around her she is agitated; if she is alone she will be calm. Quite right, she is still in there. After a while I shall approach her *en passant*; I have earned the right to make a remark, she owes me at least a greeting . . . She's sitting. Poor girl, she looks so sad. She has been crying, I think, or at least has tears in her eyes. It is outrageous making a girl like that cry. But be calm, you shall be avenged, I shall avenge you, he will learn what it means to keep her waiting. – How beautiful she is, now that the various squalls have subsided and she rests in a single mood. Her being is a harmony of sadness and pain. She really is captivating. She sits there in travelling clothes, yet it wasn't she who was to travel, she put them on so as to journey out in search of joy; now it is a sign of her pain, for she is like someone from whom gladness departs. She looks out, as though constantly taking leave of the loved one. Let him go! – The situation is favourable, the moment beckons. The thing now is to express myself in a way that makes it seem that I believed she was looking for her family or a party of friends up here, and yet warmly enough, too, for every word to be appropriate to her feelings, then I shall have a chance to worm my way into her thoughts. – Now devil take the scoundrel! If there isn't a man arriving who can only be him. No, take me for a bungler, just as I've got the situation as I wanted it. Yes, yes, something can surely be salvaged from it. I must touch upon their relationship, have myself placed in the situation. When she sees me she'll have to smile at my believing she was looking for someone quite different. That smile makes me her accomplice, which is always something. – A thousand thanks my child, that smile is worth much more to me than you think; it is the beginning, and the beginning is always the hardest. Now we are acquainted, and our acquaintance is based upon a piquant situation; it is enough to be going on with. You will hardly stay here more than an hour; within two hours I shall know who you are – why else do you think the police keep census rolls?

the 9th

Have I gone blind? Has the soul's inner eye lost its power? I have seen her, but it's as if I'd seen a heavenly revelation, so completely has her image vanished from me again. Vainly do I call upon all the strength of my soul to conjure forth this image. If ever I saw her again I'd recognize her immediately even if she stood among a hundred. Now she has run away, and my mind's eye seeks in vain to overtake her with its longing. – I was walking along

Langelinie, to all appearances unconcerned and without regard to my surroundings, although my watchful glance let nothing go unobserved, when my eye fell on her. It fixed itself unwaveringly upon her, it no longer obeyed its master's will. It was impossible for me to undertake any movement with it and use it to survey the object I would behold; I did not see, I stared. Like a fencer who freezes in his pass, so was my eye fixed, petrified in the direction it had taken. It was impossible for me to look down, impossible to withdraw my glance, impossible for me to see, because I saw far too much. The only thing I can remember is that she wore a green cape, that's all. One can call that catching the cloud instead of Juno; she has slipped away from me like Joseph from Potiphar's wife and has left only her cape behind. She was accompanied by an oldish lady, who appeared to be her mother. Her I can describe from top to toe, even though I never really saw her but at most took her in *en passant*. So it goes. The girl made an impression upon me and I have forgotten her. The other has made no impression and I can remember her.

the 11th

The same contradiction still blinds my soul. I know I have seen her, but I know also I have forgotten it again, in a way that the residue of memory left over gives no refreshment. With a restlessness and vehemence that put my well-being at risk, my soul demands this image, yet it does not appear; I could tear out my eyes to punish them for their forgetfulness. When I have finished impatiently raging, when I become calm, it is as if intimation and memory wove a picture which still cannot take definite shape because I cannot get it to stand still all at once. It is like a pattern in a fine texture; the pattern is lighter than the ground and by itself it is invisible because it is too light. – This is a curious state to be in, yet it has its pleasant side both in itself and also because it proves to me that I am still young. It can also teach me something else, namely that I'm always seeking my prey among young girls, not among young wives. A wife has less of nature in her, more coquetry; the relationship with her is not beautiful, not interesting, but piquant, and the piquant is always what comes last. I had not expected to be able to taste again the first fruits of infatuation. I am over my ears in love, I have got what swimmers call a ducking; no wonder I am a little confused. So much the better, so much the more I promise myself from this relationship.

the 14th

I hardly recognize myself. My mind rages like a sea tossed by the storms of passion. If another could see my soul in this condition, it would look as if, like a boat, it bored its bow down in the sea, as if with its fearful speed it had to plunge into the depths of the abyss. He does not see that high up on the mast there sits a sailor on lookout. Rage, you wild forces, stir your powers of passion! Even if the crashing of your waves hurls the foam to the skies, you will still not manage to pile up over my head; I sit serene as the King of the Cliff.

I can almost not find my footing, like a water-bird I seek in vain to alight on my mind's turbulent sea. And yet such turbulence is my element, I build upon it, just as *Alcedo ispida* builds its nest on the sea.

Turkey cocks puff themselves up when they see red; it's the same with me when I see green, every time I see a green cape; and since my eyes often deceive me, all my expectations are sometimes dashed on seeing a porter from Frederiks Hospital.

the 20th

One has to restrict oneself, that is a main condition of all enjoyment. It doesn't seem I can expect so soon to get any information about the girl who fills my soul and thoughts so much that they keep her loss alive. Now I shall stay quite calm, for this state I'm in, this obscure and undefined but intense unrest, has a sweet side nevertheless. I have always loved, on a moonlit night, to lie out in a boat on one of our lovely lakes. I take in the sails and the oars, remove the rudder, stretch out full-length, and gaze up into the vault of heaven. When the boat rocks on the breast of the waves, when the clouds scud before the strong wind so that the moon vanishes for a moment and then reappers, I find rest in this unrest. The motion of the waves lulls me, their lapping against the boat is a monotonous cradle-song. The swift flight of the clouds, the shifting light and shadow, intoxicate me so that I am in a waking dream. Thus now, too, I lay myself out, take in the sails and rudder; longing and impatient expectation toss me about in their arms; longing and expectation become more and more quiet, more and more blissful, they fondle me like a child; the heaven of hope arches over me; her image floats by me like the moon's, indistinct, blinding me now with its light, now with its shadow. How enjoyable thus to splash up and down on a stormy lake – how enjoyable to be stirred in oneself.

the 21st

The days go by and I am no nearer. Young girls give me pleasure more than ever and still I have no desire to enjoy them. I seek her everywhere. It often makes me unreasonable, blurs my vision, enervates my pleasure. That beautiful season is soon coming now when, in public life in the streets and lanes, one buys up these small favours which, in the winter's social life, one can pay dearly enough for, for although there is much a young girl can forget, she cannot forget a situation. Social life does indeed bring one in contact with the fair sex, but there is no artistry in starting an affair there. In social life every young girl is armed, the occasion is threadbare and repeated over and over again; she gets no voluptuous thrill. In the street she is on the open sea and everything therefore seems more intense; it is as if there were mystery in everything. I would give a hundred dollars for a smile from a young girl in a street situation, but not even ten for a handclasp at a party; these are currencies of quite different kinds. Once the affair is under way, you can then seek out the person in question at parties. You have a secret communication with her that tempts you, and it is the most effective stimulant I know. She dares not speak of it and yet she thinks of it; she doesn't know if you've forgotten it or not; you lead her astray in one way and then another. Probably I shan't collect much this year; this girl preoccupies me too much. In a sense my returns will be poor; but then I have the prospect of the big prize.

the 5th

Damned chance! I have never cursed you for appearing, I curse you because you don't appear at all. Or is this perhaps some new invention of yours, you unfathomable being, barren mother of all that exists, sole remnant of that time when necessity gave birth to freedom, when freedom let itself be duped back into its mother's womb? Damned chance! You, my only confidant, the only being I consider worthy to be my ally and my enemy, always the same however different, always unfathomable, always a riddle! You, whom I love with all the sympathy in my soul, in whose image I form myself, why do you not appear? I am not begging, I do not humbly entreat you to appear in this way or that; such worship would be idolatry, not well-pleasing to you. I challenge you to battle: why don't you appear? Or has the turbulence in the world's structure come to a standstill? Is your riddle solved, so that you too have plunged into the ocean of eternity? Terrible thought, for then the world has come to a standstill from boredom! Damned chance! I am waiting for you. I do not wish to defeat you with principles, or with what foolish people call character; no, I want to be your poet! I'll not be a poet for others. Show yourself! I compose you, I consume my own verse and it is my sustenance. Or do you find me unworthy? As a bayadère dances to the honour of God, I have dedicated myself to your service; light, thinly clad, supple, unarmed, I renounce everything, I own nothing, I have no mind to own anything, I love nothing, I have nothing to lose; but haven't I then become more worthy of you, you who long ago must have wearied of depriving people of what they loved, wearied of their cowardly sighs and prayers? Take me by surprise, I am ready, no stakes, let us fight for honour. Show me her, show me a possibility that looks like an impossibility; show me her in the shadows of the underworld, I shall fetch her up. Let her hate me, despise me, be indifferent to me, love another, I'm not afraid; but stir up the waters, break your silence. It's cheap of you to starve me in this way, you who after all fancy yourself stronger than I.

May 6th

Spring is at hand. Everything is in bloom, including the young girls. Capes are laid aside, and presumably my green one has been hung up. That's what comes of making a girl's acquaintance in the street instead of at a party, where one finds out immediately what she is called, what family she is from, where she lives, whether she is engaged. This last is extremely important for all steadfast and sober-minded suitors, to whom it would never occur to fall in love with a girl who was engaged. Such an easy-paced ambler would be in deadly peril if he were in my place; he would be completely devastated if his efforts to acquire information were crowned with success, with the bonus that she was engaged. But that doesn't worry me much. An engaged girl is only a comic difficulty. I have no fear either of comic or of tragic difficulties; all I fear are the tediously long-drawn-out ones. So far I haven't secured a single piece of information, in spite of surely leaving no stone unturned and often feeling the truth of the poet's words:

> *Nox et hiems longaeque viae, saevique dolores*
> *mollibus his castris, et labor omnis inest.*

Perhaps after all she doesn't live here in town, perhaps she is from the country, perhaps, perhaps – I could go crazy over all these perhapses, and the more crazy I become, the more perhapses. I always have money in readiness for a journey. In vain I look for her at the theatre, at concerts, ballets, and on promenades. That pleases me in a way; a young girl who takes too much part in such entertainments is generally not worth conquering; she usually lacks that originality which for me is a *sine qua non*. One can more easily imagine finding a Preciosa among the gypsies than in the cheap dancing-halls where young girls are put up for sale – in all innocence, of course, Lord preserve us, what else?

*

Yes, my child, why didn't you stay standing quite still at the door? There is nothing at all reprehensible about a young girl's stopping in a doorway when it's raining. I do the same sometimes when I have no umbrella, sometimes even when I have, as for instance now. Besides, I could mention a number of respectable ladies who have not hesitated to do so. You have only to stand quietly, turn your back to the street, so that passers-by can't tell whether you are standing there or are about to go into the house. On the other hand, it is unwise to hide oneself behind the door when it is half open, mainly because of the consequences; for the more you are hidden, the more unpleasant it is to be surprised. But if you do hide, you should stand quite still, committing yourself to the good genie and the custody of all the angels; you should particularly refrain from peeping out – to see if it has stopped raining. If you want to find out, then step out boldly and look earnestly up into the sky. But if you poke your head out a little curiously, shyly, anxiously, uncertainly, and then hurriedly draw it in again – then every child understands that movement; it's called playing hide-and-seek. And I, who always take part, I should of course hold back and not answer when asked . . . Don't think I'm getting any injurious ideas, you hadn't the slightest intention when you poked out your head, it was the most innocent thing in the world. In return you mustn't get ideas about me, my good name and reputation won't stand it. Besides, it was you who started it. I advise you never to tell anyone of this; you were in the wrong. What else can I do other than what any gentleman would – offer you my umbrella? – Where has she got to? Excellent, she has hidden herself in the porter's doorway. – She is a most charming little girl, merry, pleased. – 'Do you know anything of a young lady who just a blessed moment ago poked her head out of this doorway, evidently in need of an umbrella? It is she I am looking for, I and my umbrella.' – You laugh – perhaps you will allow me to send my servant to fetch it tomorrow, or if you ask me to call a carriage – nothing to thank me for, it is only due courtesy. – She is one of the most joyful girls I have seen in a long time, her glance is so childlike and yet so forthright, her nature so charming, so pure, and yet she is curious. – Go in peace, my child, if it were not for a certain green cape, I might have wanted to make a closer acquaintance. – She walks down to Købmagergade. How innocent and trusting, not a sign of prudery. Look how lightly she walks, how gaily she tosses her head – the green cape demands self-denial.

the 15th

Thank you, kind chance, accept my thanks! Straight she was and proud, mysterious and rich in ideas as a spruce, a shoot, a thought, which from deep in the earth sprouts up towards heaven, unexplained and to itself inexplicable, a whole that has no parts. The beech crowns itself, its leaves tell of what has taken place beneath; the spruce has no crown, no history, a mystery to itself – such was she. She was hidden from herself inside herself, she rose up from out of herself, she had a self-contained pride, like the daring flight of the spruce, even though it is fastened to the earth. A sadness poured over her like the cooing of the woodpigeon, a deep longing that had no want. She was a riddle, who mysteriously possessed her own solution, a secret, and what are all diplomats' secrets compared with this, an enigma, and what in all the world beautiful as the word that solves it? How significant, how to solve' [*at løse*], what ambiguity it contains, combinations where this word partly because everything suggests transience and vanity, and evokes an impatience that makes the enjoyment less soothing. At times I would not wish to dispense with the ballroom, I would not forgo its costly luxury, its priceless abundance of youth and beauty, its manifold play of forces; but then it isn't so much that I enjoy myself as gorge myself in possibility. It is not a single beauty that captivates me but a totality; a dream image floats past, in which all these feminine natures form their own configurations among one another, and all these movements seek something, seek rest in one picture that is not seen.

It was on the path between Nørre- and Østerport, about half-past six. The sun had lost its strength, its memory only was preserved in a mild radiance spreading over the landscape. Nature breathed more freely. The lake was calm, smooth as a mirror. The comfortable houses on Blegdammen were reflected in the water, which further out was dark as metal. The path and the buildings on the other side were lit by the faint rays of the sun. The sky was clear and only a single light cloud floated over it unnoticed, best seen by directing your eyes at the lake, over whose shining forehead it vanished from view. Not a leaf moved. – It was her. My eye did not deceive me, even though the green cape had done so. In sp— of being prepared now for so long, it was impossible to c— certain excitement, a rising and falling, li— that rose and fell in the adjacent

childlike and yet so forthright, her nature so charming, so pure, and yet she is curious. – Go in peace, my child, if it were not for a certain green cape, I might have wanted to make a closer acquaintance. – She walks down to Købmagergade. How innocent and trusting, not a sign of prudery. Look how lightly she walks, how gaily she tosses her head – the green cape demands self-denial.

the 15th

Thank you, kind chance, accept my thanks! Straight she was and proud, mysterious and rich in ideas as a spruce, a shoot, a thought, which from deep in the earth sprouts up towards heaven, unexplained and to itself inexplicable, a whole that has no parts. The beech crowns itself, its leaves tell of what has taken place beneath; the spruce has no crown, no history, a mystery to itself – such was she. She was hidden from herself inside herself, she rose up from out of herself, she had a self-contained pride, like the daring flight of the spruce, even though it is fastened to the earth. A sadness poured over her like the cooing of the woodpigeon, a deep longing that had no want. She was a riddle, who mysteriously possessed her own solution, a secret, and what are all diplomats' secrets compared with this, an enigma, and what in all the world is so beautiful as the word that solves it? How significant, how pregnant, language is: 'to solve' [*at løse*], what ambiguity it contains, how beautiful and strong in all the combinations where this word appears! As the wealth of the soul is a riddle, as long as the ligature of the tongue is not loosed [*løst*], and the riddle thereby solved [*løst*], so is a young girl, too, a riddle. – Thank you, kind chance, accept my thanks! If I had seen her first in winter she'd have been wrapped in that green cape, frozen perhaps and, in her, Nature's inclemency might have diminished its own beauty. But now, what luck! I saw her first at the most beautiful time of year, in the spring, in the light of late afternoon. True, winter also has its advantages. A brilliantly lit ballroom can indeed be a flattering setting for a young girl in evening dress. But she seldom appears to best advantage here, partly because everything demands it of her, a demand whose effect is disturbing whether she gives in to it or resists, and

partly because everything suggests transience and vanity, and evokes an impatience that makes the enjoyment less soothing. At times I would not wish to dispense with the ballroom, I would not forgo its costly luxury, its priceless abundance of youth and beauty, its manifold play of forces; but then it isn't so much that I enjoy myself as gorge myself in possibility. It is not a single beauty that captivates me but a totality; a dream image floats past, in which all these feminine natures form their own configurations among one another, and all these movements seek something, seek rest in one picture that is not seen.

It was on the path between Nørre- and Østerport, about half-past six. The sun had lost its strength, its memory only was preserved in a mild radiance spreading over the landscape. Nature breathed more freely. The lake was calm, smooth as a mirror. The comfortable houses on Blegdammen were reflected in the water, which further out was dark as metal. The path and the buildings on the other side were lit by the faint rays of the sun. The sky was clear and only a single light cloud floated over it unnoticed, best seen by directing your eyes at the lake, over whose shining forehead it vanished from view. Not a leaf moved. – It was her. My eye did not deceive me, even though the green cape had done so. In spite of being prepared now for so long, it was impossible to control a certain excitement, a rising and falling, like the song of the lark that rose and fell in the adjacent fields. She was alone. How she was dressed I have forgotten again, and yet now I have a picture of her. She was alone, preoccupied, evidently not with herself but with her thoughts. She was not thinking, but the quiet pursuit of her thoughts wove a picture of longing before her soul, possessed by presentiment, inexplicably like a young girl's many sighs. She was at her most beautiful age. A young girl does not develop in the sense that a boy does; she does not grow, she is born. A boy begins straightaway to develop, and it takes a long time; a young girl takes a long time being born and is born full-grown. Therein lies her infinite richness; the moment she is born she is fully grown, but this moment of birth comes late. Therefore she is born twice, the second time when she marries, or, rather, at that moment she

ceases being born, that is her moment of birth. It is not just Minerva who sprang fully grown from the head of Jupiter, not just Venus who rose from the ocean in all her beauty; every young girl is like this if her womanliness has not been destroyed by what people call development. She awakens not by degrees but all at once; on the other hand, she dreams all the longer, provided people are not so unreasonable as to arouse her too early. But this dream is an infinite richness. – She was preoccupied not with herself but in herself, and in her this preoccupation was an infinite peace and repose. This is how a young girl is rich; encompassing this richness makes oneself rich. She is rich even though she does not know that she owns anything. She is rich, she is a treasure. A quiet peacefulness brooded over her and a little sadness. She was light to lift up with the eyes, as light as Psyche who was carried off by genies, lighter still, for she carried herself. Let theologians dispute on the Virgin Mary's Assumption; to me it seems not inconceivable, for she no longer belonged to the world; but the lightness of a young girl is incomprehensible and makes mockery of the law of gravity. – She noticed nothing and therefore believed herself unnoticed. I kept my distance and absorbed her image. She was walking slowly, no urgency disturbed her peace or the quiet of her surroundings. By the lake sat a boy fishing, she stopped and looked at the mirror surface of the water and the small river. Although she had not been walking vigorously she sought to cool herself. She loosened a little kerchief fastened about her neck under her shawl. A soft breeze from the lake fanned a bosom as white as snow, yet warm and full. The boy seemed unhappy to have a witness to his catch; he turned to her with a somewhat phlegmatic glance and watched her. He really cut a ridiculous figure, and I cannot blame her for beginning to laugh at him. How youthfully she laughed! If she had been alone with the boy I don't think she would have been afraid of coming to blows with him. Her eyes were large and radiant; when one looked into them they had a dark lustre which, because of their impenetrability, gave a hint of their infinite depth; they were pure and innocent, gentle and quiet, full of mischief when she smiled. Her nose was finely arched; when I saw her sideways it seemed to merge with the forehead, making it a little shorter and a little more spirited. She walked on, I followed. Happily there were many strollers on the path; while exchanging a few words with some of them, I let her gain a little on me and soon overtook her again, thus relieving myself of the need to keep my distance by walking as slowly as she did. She walked in the direction of Østerport. I wished to see her more closely without being seen. At the corner stood a house from which that might be possible. I knew the family and so needed only to call on them. I hurried past her at a good pace, as though paying her not the slightest heed. I got a good lead on her, greeted the family right and left, and then took possession of the window which overlooked the path. She came, I looked and looked while at the same time keeping up a conversation with the tea party in the drawing-room. The way she walked easily convinced me she hadn't taken many dancing lessons, yet it had a pride, a natural nobility, but an artlessness. I had another opportunity to see her that I really had not reckoned with. From the window I could not see very far down the path, but I could see a jetty extending out into the lake, and to my great surprise, I discovered her again out there. It occurred to me that perhaps she belonged out here in the country; maybe the family had summer rooms. I was already on the point of regretting my call, for fear that she might turn back so that I would lose sight of her; indeed, the fact that she could be seen at the extreme end of the jetty was a sort of sign that she was disappearing from my view – when she appeared close by. She had gone past the house; in great haste I seized my hat and cane in order, if possible, to walk past and then lag behind her several times again until I found out where she lived – when in my haste I jostled the arm of a lady about to serve tea. A frightful screaming arose. I stood there with my hat and cane and, anxious only to get away and if possible give a twist to the matter to motivate my retreat, I exclaimed with great feeling, 'Like Cain I shall be banished from the place where this tea was spilled.' But as if everything conspired against me, the host conceived the desperate idea of following up my remarks and declared, loudly and solemnly, that I was forbidden to leave before I had enjoyed a cup of tea;

I myself served the ladies the tea I had deprived them of, and thus made good everything once more. Since I was perfectly certain that my host, under the circumstances, would consider it a courtesy to use force, there was nothing for it but to remain. – She had vanished.

the 16th

How beautiful to be in love, how interesting to know one is in love! See, that's the difference! The thought of her disappearing a second time can be irritating but in a sense it pleases me. The picture I now have of her wavers indeterminately between being her actual and her ideal image. I am now evoking it, but precisely because either it is real or it has at least its source in reality, it has its own fascination. I feel no impatience, since she must belong here in town, and for me that is enough for the moment. It is this possibility that makes her image properly appear – everything should be savoured in slow draughts. And should I not indeed be relaxed, I who consider myself the darling of the gods, to whom befell the rare good fortune to fall in love again? That, after all, is something no art, no study, can produce; it is a gift. But since I have succeeded in stirring up a love once more, I want at least to see how long it can be kept going. This love I coddle as I never did my first. Such an opportunity is not given every day, it seems, so it is truly a matter of making the most of it. That's what drives one to despair. Seducing a girl is no art, but it needs a stroke of good fortune to find one worth seducing. – Love has many mysteries, and this first infatuation is also a mystery, even if a minor one – most people who rush into it get engaged or indulge in other foolish pranks, and then it's all over in the twinkling of an eye and they don't know what they have conquered or what they have lost. Twice now she has appeared before me and vanished; that means that soon she will appear more frequently. After he has interpreted Pharaoh's dream, Joseph adds: 'The fact that you dreamt this twice, means that it will soon come to pass.'

Still, it would be interesting if one could see a little in advance those forces whose coming on the scene makes for life's content.

She lives her life now in peace and quiet; she has no suspicion I even exist, even less what goes on inside me, less still the certainty with which I survey her future; for my soul demands more and more reality, it is becoming stronger and stronger. When, at a first glance, a girl does not make a deep enough impression upon one to awaken the ideal, then the real thing is usually not particularly desirable. But if she does awaken it, then however experienced one may be, generally one is a little overwhelmed. But for someone uncertain of his hand, his eye and his victory, I would always advise him to chance an attack at this first stage when, just because he is overwhelmed, he is in possession of extraordinary powers. For this being overwhelmed is a curious mixture of sympathy and egoism. On the other hand, he will forgo an enjoyment because he does not enjoy a situation he himself is secretly involved in. What is nicest is hard to decide; what the most interesting, easy. However, it is always good to get as close to the limit as possible. That is the real pleasure and what others enjoy I've no idea. The mere possession isn't much and the means lovers use are generally wretched enough; they even stoop to money, power, influence, sleeping draughts, and so on. But what pleasure can there be in love when it is not the most absolute self-surrender, that is, on the one side? But that as a rule requires spirit, and as a rule these lovers lack that.

the 19th

So her name is Cordelia. Cordelia! That's a pretty name, which is also important, since often it is very disconcerting to have to use an ugly name in connection with the tenderest attributions. I recognized her a long way off; she was walking with two other girls on her left. The way they walked suggested they would soon be stopping. I stood at the corner and read a poster while keeping a constant eye on my unknown. They took leave of one another. The two had presumably come a little out of their way, since they took an opposite direction. She set off towards my corner. When she had taken a few steps, one of the other girls came running after her, calling loudly enough for me to hear, 'Cordelia! Cordelia!' Then the third girl came up; they put their heads together for a private conference, which with my keenest ear I tried in vain to hear. Then all three laughed and went off in rather greater haste in the direction the two had taken before. I followed. They went into a house on the Strand. I waited quite a time since it seemed likely that Cordelia would soon return alone. But that didn't happen.

Cordelia! That is really an excellent name; it was also the name of the third of King Lear's daughters, that remarkable girl whose heart did not dwell upon her lips, whose lips were silent when her heart was full. So too with my Cordelia. She resembles her, of that I'm certain. But in another sense her heart does dwell upon her lips, not in words but more cordially in the form of a kiss. How full of health her lips were! Never have I seen prettier.

That I am really in love I can tell among other things by the secrecy, almost even to myself, with which I treat this matter. All love is secretive, even faithless love when it has the necessary aesthetic element. It has never occurred to me to want confidants or boast of my affairs. So it was almost gratifying not to get to know her address but a place that she frequents. Besides, perhaps because of this I have come even nearer to my goal. I can begin my investigations without attracting her attention, and from this fixed point it shouldn't be difficult to gain access to her family. Should that prove difficult, however, *eh bien*; it's all in the day's work; everything I do I do *con amore*; and thus also I love *con amore*.

the 20th

Today I got hold of some information about the house she disappeared into. It's a widow with three blessed daughters. An abundance of information can be got from that source, that's if they have any. The only difficulty is to understand this information when raised to the third power, since all three talk at once. She is called Cordelia Wahl, and she is the daughter of a Navy captain. He died some years ago, and the mother too. He was a very hard and strict husband. Now she lives in the house with her aunt, her father's sister, who is said to resemble her brother but is a very respectable woman besides. So far so good, but beyond that they know nothing of this house; they never go there, but Cordelia often visits them. She and the two girls are taking a course at the Royal Kitchens. She usually goes there in the afternoon, sometimes also in the morning, never in the evening. They live a very secluded life.

So that's the end of the story. There seems to be no bridge by which I can slip over into Cordelia's house.

She has, then, some conception of life's pains, of its darker side. Who would have thought it of her? Still, these memories belong to her earlier years; it is a horizon she has lived under without really noticing it. That's a very good thing; it has saved her womanliness, she is not crippled. It can be useful, on the other hand, for raising her to a higher level, if one knows how to bring it out. All such things usually produce pride, in so far as they don't crush, and certainly she is far from being crushed.

the 21st

She lives by the ramparts; it isn't one of the best localities, no neighbours over the way for me to strike up acquaintance with, no public places from which I could make my observations unnoticed. The ramparts themselves are hardly suitable: one is too visible. If one goes down to the street, the other side right by the ramparts, that will hardly do, for no one goes there and it would be too conspicuous, or else one would have to go along the side on which the houses front and then one can't see anything. It's a corner house. From the street one can also see the windows to the courtyard, since there is no neighbouring house. That is presumably where her bedroom is.

the 22nd

Today I saw her for the first time at Mrs Jansen's. I was introduced. She didn't seem much concerned, or to take much note of me. I behaved as unobtrusively as possible to be the more attentive. She stayed only a moment, she had merely called to fetch the daughters, who were due to go to the Royal Kitchens. While the two Jansen girls were getting on their wraps, we two were alone in the drawing-room, and I made a few cool, almost nonchalant remarks to her, which were returned with undeserved courtesy.

Then they left. I could have offered to accompany them, but that would have been enough to mark me down as a ladies' man, and I am convinced she cannot be won in that way. – I preferred, instead, to leave a moment after they had gone but considerably faster than they and by another street, though still aiming at the Royal Kitchens, so that just as they turned into Store Kongensgade I rushed past them in great haste, without greeting or anything, to their great astonishment.

the 23rd

I have to gain access to the house, and for that I am, in military parlance, at the ready. However, it looks like being a long-drawn-out and difficult affair. Never have I known a family that lived so isolated. There are only herself and her aunt. No brothers, no cousins, not a shred to seize on, no relatives however distant to walk arm-in-arm with. I go about with one arm constantly hanging free; not for the whole world would I take someone by the arm at this time. My arm is a grapnel which must always be kept in readiness; it is designed for unexpected returns, in case far off in the distance there should appear a remote relative or friend, whom from that distance I could take lightly by the arm – then clamber aboard. But in any case, it is wrong of the family to live so isolated; one deprives the poor girl of the opportunity to get to know the world, to say nothing of what other dangerous consequences it may have. It never pays. That goes for courting too. Such isolation may well protect one against petty thievery; in a very hospitable house opportunity makes the thief. But that doesn't mean much, for from girls of that kind there isn't much to steal; when they are sixteen their hearts are already completed samplers and I have never cared to write my name where others have already written. It never occurs to me to scratch my name on a windowpane or in an inn, or on a tree or a bench in Frederiksberg Gardens.

the 27th

The more I see her, the more I am convinced she is a very isolated figure. A man should never be that, not even a young one, for since reflection is essential to his development he must have come into contact with others. But for that reason a girl should rather not be interesting, for the interesting always contains a reflection upon itself, just as the interesting in art always gives you the artist too. A young girl who wants to please by being interesting really only succeeds in pleasing herself. This is the aesthetic objection to all forms of coquetry. All the figurative coquetry which forms part of natural motion is another matter, for instance feminine modesty, which is always the most delightful coquetry. An interesting girl may indeed succeed in pleasing, but just as she has herself renounced her femininity, so also are the men she pleases usually correspondingly effeminate. A young girl of this kind really only becomes interesting through her relationship to men. Woman is the weaker sex, and yet for her, much more than for the man, it is essential to be alone with herself in her younger years. She must be sufficient unto herself, but what she is sufficient in and through is an illusion; it is the dowry that Nature has bestowed on her, as with the daughter of a king. But it is just this resting in illusion that isolates her. I have often wondered why nothing is more demoralizing for a young girl than constant association with other young girls. Evidently, it is due to that association being neither one thing nor the other. It disturbs the illusion but doesn't bring light to it. Woman's highest destiny is to be a companion to the man, but association with her own sex causes a reflection to focus upon this association, and instead of becoming a companion she becomes a lady's companion. Language itself has much to say in this respect. The man is called Master but the woman is not called Handmaiden or anything of that sort; no, an essential qualification is used, she is a 'companion', not a 'companioness'. If I were to imagine my ideal of a girl, she would always have to stand alone in the world and therefore be left to herself, but especially not have girl friends. True, the Graces were three, but surely it has never occurred to anyone to imagine them conversing with one another; in their silent trinity they form a beautiful feminine unity. In this respect I might almost be tempted to recommend the return of the lady's bower, were this constraint not also injurious. It is always most desirable for a young girl to be allowed her freedom but no opportunity offered her. This makes her beautiful and saves her from being interesting. It is in vain to give a young girl who has spent a great deal of time with other girls a maiden's veil or a bridal veil; on the other hand, a man with enough aesthetic appreciation always finds that a girl who is innocent in a deeper and truer sense is brought to him veiled, even if bridal veils are not in fashion.

She has been brought up strictly; I honour her parents in their graves for that. She lives a very reserved life, and for that I could fall on her aunt's neck in gratitude. She is not yet acquainted with the pleasures of the world, does not have the chattering surfeit. She is proud, she defies what other young girls find pleasure in. That's as it should be; it is an untruth which I shall know how to work to my profit. She takes no pleasure in ceremony and fuss as other young girls do; she is a little polemical, but that is necessary for a young girl with her enthusiasms. She lives in the world of imagination. Were she to fall into the wrong hands, it might bring something very unwomanly out of her, precisely because there is so much womanliness in her.

the 30th

Everywhere our paths cross. Today I met her three times. I know of her every little excursion, when and where I shall come across her. But this knowledge is not used to secure a meeting. On the contrary, I squander on a frightful scale. A meeting which often has cost me several hours' waiting is thrown away as a trifle. I do not meet her, I merely touch tangentially upon the periphery of her existence. If I know she is going to Mrs Jansen's I prefer not to arrive there at the same time, unless it is important for me to carry out some particular observation. I prefer arriving a little early at Mrs Jansen's, and then if possible meeting her at the door as she is coming and I am leaving, or on the steps where I run unheedingly past her. This is the first net she must be spun into. I do not stop her on the street, or I might exchange a greeting but always keep my distance. She must certainly be struck by our continual encounters; no doubt she notices that a new body has appeared on her horizon, whose movement in a curiously undisturbing way has a disturbing effect on her own, but of the law governing this movement she has no idea. To look for its point of attraction her inclination is rather to look right and left; that she is herself that point she is no more the wiser than her polar opposite. With her it is as with those with whom I associate in general, they believe I have a multiplicity of affairs; I am continually on the go and say, like Figaro, 'One, two, three, four intrigues at once, that's my delight.' I must get to know her first and her whole state of mind before beginning my assault. Most men enjoy a young girl as they do a glass of champagne, in a single frothing moment; oh, yes! that's really nice, and with many young girls it's no doubt the most one can make of it. But here there is more. If the individual is too frail to stand clarity and transparency, well then, one enjoys obscurity, but she can obviously stand it. The more surrender one can bring into love, the more interesting it becomes. This momentary pleasure is a case of rape, if not in an outward sense at least spiritually, and in rape there is only an imaginary pleasure; it is like a stolen kiss, something with no substance behind it. No, when one brings matters to the point where a girl has just one task to accomplish for her freedom, to surrender herself, when she feels her whole bliss depends on that, when she almost begs to submit and yet is free, then for the first time there is enjoyment, but it always depends on a spiritual influence.

Cordelia! What a glorious name. I sit at home and practise it like a parrot. I say 'Cordelia, Cordelia, my Cordelia, my own Cordelia'. I can scarcely forbear smiling at the thought of the routine with which I will come, at a decisive moment, to utter these words. One should always make preliminary studies, everything must be properly prepared. It is no wonder that the poets always portray this intimate moment, this beautiful moment, when the lovers, not content with being sprinkled (sure enough, there are many who never get further), but descending into love's ocean divest themselves of the old person and climb up from this baptism, only now, for the first time, properly knowing each other as old acquaintances though only an instant old. For a young girl this is always the most beautiful moment, and properly to savour it one should always be a little higher, so that one is not only the one being baptized but also the priest. A little irony makes this moment's second moment one of the most interesting; it is a spiritual undressing. One must be poet enough not to disturb the ceremony yet the joker must always be sitting in ambush.

June 2nd

She is proud; I have seen that for a long time. When she sits together with the three Jansens she talks very little, their chatter obviously bores her, and certainly the smile on her lips seems to indicate that. I am counting on that smile. – At other times she can surrender herself to an almost boyish wildness, to the great surprise of the Jansens. For me it is not inexplicable when I consider her childhood. She had only one brother, who was a year older. She knew only her father and brother, had been a witness to serious scenes which produce a distaste in general for jabber. Her father and mother had not lived happily together; what usually beckons, more or less clearly or vaguely, to a young girl does not beckon to her. She may possibly be puzzled about what it means to be a young girl. Perhaps at times she wished she were not a girl but a man.

She has imagination, soul, passion, in short, all substantial qualities, but not in a subjectively reflected form. A chance occurrence convinced me of that today. I gathered from Jansen & Co. that she did not play the piano, it is against her aunt's principles. I have always regretted that attitude, for music is always a good avenue for communicating with a young girl, if one takes care, be it noted, not to pose as a connoisseur. Today I went to Mrs Jansen's. I had half opened the door without knocking, an impertinence that has often stood me in good stead, and which, when necessary, I remedy with a bit of ridicule by knocking on the open door. She sat alone at the piano – she seemed to be playing on the sly (it was a little Swedish melody) – she was not an accomplished player, she became impatient, but then gentler sounds came again. I closed the door and stood outside, listening to the change in her moods; there was sometimes a passion in her playing which reminds one of the maiden Mittelil, who struck the golden harp with such vigour that milk gushed from her breasts. – There was something melancholy but also something dithyrambic in her execution. – I might have rushed in, seized the moment – that would have been foolish. – Memory is not just a preservative but also a means of enhancement; what is permeated by memory seems doubled. – In books, especially in psalters, one often finds a little flower – some beautiful moment has furnished the occasion for preserving it, and yet the memory is even more beautiful. She is evidently concealing the fact that she plays, or perhaps she plays only this little Swedish melody – has it perhaps a special interest for her? All this I do not know, but the incident is for that reason very important to me. Whenever I can talk more confidentially with her, I shall lead her quite secretly to this point and let her fall into this trap.

June 3rd

I still cannot decide how she is to be understood. I wait therefore as quietly, as inconspicuously – yes, as a soldier in a cordon of scouts who throws himself to the ground to listen for the most distant sound of an approaching enemy. I do not really exist for her, not in the sense of a negative relationship, but of no relationship at all. Still I have not dared any experiment. To see her and love her were the same – that's what it says in romances – yes, it is true enough, if love had no dialectic; but what does one really learn about love from romances? Sheer lies that help to shorten the task.

When I think now, with the information I have gained, back upon the impression the first meeting made upon me, I'd say that my ideas about her have changed, but as much to her advantage as to mine. It isn't quite the order of the day for a young girl to go out so much alone or for a young girl to be so self-absorbed. She was tested according to my strict critique and found: delightful. But delight is a very fleeting factor which vanishes like yesterday when that day is gone. I had not imagined her in the setting in which she lived, least of all so unreflectingly familiar with life's storms.

I wonder how it is with her emotions. She has certainly never been in love, her spirit is too free-soaring for that; least of all is she one of those virgins experienced in theory who, well before the time, can so fluently imagine being in the arms of a loved one. The real-life figures she has met with have been less than such as to confuse her about the relation of dreams to reality. Her soul is still nourished by the divine ambrosia of ideals. But the ideal that floats before her is hardly a shepherdess or a heroine in a romance, a mistress; it is a Jeanne d'Arc or some such.

The question is always whether her femininity is strong enough to reflect itself; or whether it is only to be enjoyed as beauty and charm. The question is whether one dares to tense the bow more strongly. It is a wonderful thing in itself to find a pure immediate femininity, but risking change gives you the interesting; in which case the best thing is simply to saddle her with a suitor. There is a superstition that this would harm a young girl. – Indeed, if she is a very refined and delicate plant with just the one outstanding quality, charm, the best thing for her would be never to have heard of love. But if this is not the case it is an advantage, and I would never have scruples about getting hold of a suitor if none is at hand. Nor must this suitor be a caricature, for then nothing is gained; he must be a respectable young man, if possible even amiable, but too little for her passion. She looks down on such a man, she acquires a distaste for love, she almost despairs of her own reality when she senses what she might be and sees what reality offers. If this is love, she says, it's nothing to get excited about. She becomes proud in her love, this pride makes her interesting, it transfigures her being with a higher incarnation; but she is also nearer her downfall – all of which only makes her more and more interesting. However, it is best to check her acquaintances first to see whether there might not be such a suitor. At home there is no opportunity, for next to no one comes there, but she does go out and there could well be one. Getting hold of one before knowing this is always a risky matter. Two individually insignificant suitors could have an injurious effect by their relativity. I must find out now whether there isn't such a lover sitting in secret, lacking the courage to storm the citadel, a chicken-thief who sees no opportunity in such a cloistered house.

The strategic principle then, the law of all motion in this campaign, is always to involve her in an interesting situation. The interesting is the field on which this conflict must constantly be waged, the potentialities of the interesting are to be exhausted. Unless I am quite mistaken, this is what her whole being is based on, so what I demand is just what she herself offers, indeed, what she demands. Everything depends on spying out what the individual has to offer and what, as a consequence, she demands. My love affairs therefore always have a reality for me, they form an element in my life, a creative period, of which I am fully aware; often they even involve some or other acquired skill. I learned to dance for the first girl I loved; for a little dancer's sake I learned French. At that time, like all blockheads, I went to the market-place and was frequently made a fool of. Now I go in for pre-market purchasing. But perhaps she has exhausted one aspect of the interesting; her secluded life seems to indicate that. Now it is a matter of finding another aspect which seems to her at first sight not at all interesting, but which, just because of this resistance, will become so. For this purpose I select not the poetic but the prosaic. That then is the start. First her femininity is neutralized by prosaic common sense and ridicule, not directly but indirectly, together with what is absolutely neutral: spirit. She comes close to losing the sense of her femininity, but in this condition she cannot stand alone; she throws herself into my arms, not as if I were a lover, no, still quite neutrally. Then her femininity awakens, one coaxes it to its greatest resilience, one lets her come up against something effectively real, she goes beyond it, her femininity attains almost supernatural heights, she belongs to me with a worldly passion.

the 5th

I did not have to go far. She visits at the home of Baxter, the wholesaler. Here I found not only Cordelia, but also a person just as opportune. Edvard, the son of the house, is head over heels in love with her, one needs only half of one eye to see it in both of his. He is in trade, in his father's office; a good-looking young man, quite pleasant, rather shy, which last I suspect does not hurt him in her eyes.

Poor Edvard! He simply doesn't know how to tackle his love. When he knows she is there in the evening he dresses up just for her, puts on his new dark suit just for her, cuff-links just for her, and cuts an almost ridiculous figure among the otherwise commonplace company in the drawing-room. His embarrassment borders on the unbelievable. If it were a pose, Edvard would become a very dangerous rival. Awkwardness has to be used very expertly, but with it one can come a long way. How often have I used it to fool some little virgin! Girls generally speak very harshly about awkward men, yet secretly they like them. A little embarrassment always flatters a young girl's vanity, she feels her superiority, it is change in the hand. Then when you have lulled them to sleep, you find an occasion on which they are made to believe you are about to die of embarrassment, to show that, far from it, you can quite well shift for yourself. Embarrassment deprives you of your masculine importance, and it is therefore a relatively good way of neutralizing sexual difference. So when they realize that it is only a pose, ashamed they blush inwardly, they are very conscious of having gone too far; it's as though they had gone on treating a boy too long as a child.

the 7th

We are firm friends now, Edvard and I; there exists a true friendship between us, a beautiful relationship, the like of which has not occurred since the finest days of the Greeks. We soon became intimates when, having embroiled him in diverse observations concerning Cordelia, I got him to confess his secret. When all secrets assemble, it goes without saying that this one can come along too. Poor fellow, he has already sighed for a long time. He dresses up every time she comes, then escorts her home in the evening, his heart throbs at the thought that her arm is resting on his, they walk home gazing at the stars, he rings her bell, she disappears, he despairs – but hopes for next time. He still hasn't had the courage to set his foot over her threshold, he who has so excellent an opportunity. Although I cannot refrain inwardly from making fun of Edvard, there is something nice about his child-likeness. Although ordinarily I fancy myself fairly experienced in the whole quintessence of the erotic, I have never observed this state in myself, this lovesick fear and trembling, or not to the extent that it removes my self-possession; I know it well enough in other ways, but in my case it tends to make me stronger. One might perhaps say that in that case I've never been in love. Perhaps. I have taken Edvard to task, I have encouraged him to rely on my friendship. Tomorrow he is going to take a decisive step: go in person and invite her out. I have led him to the desperate idea of begging me to go with him; I have promised to do so. He takes this to be an extraordinary display of friendship. The occasion is exactly as I would have it: we burst in on her in the drawing-room. Should she have the slightest doubt as to the meaning of my conduct, this will once more confuse everything.

Hitherto I have not been accustomed to preparing myself for my conversation; now it has become a necessity in order to entertain the aunt. I have taken on the honourable task of conversing with her to cover up Edvard's infatuated advances to Cordelia. The aunt has previously lived in the country, and through a combination of my own painstaking studies in the agronomic literature and the aunt's reports of her practical experience, I am making significant progress in insight and efficiency.

With the aunt I am totally successful; she considers me a steady, reliable man with whom it is a decided pleasure to have dealings, unlike our dandies. With Cordelia I seem not to be particularly in favour. No doubt her femininity is of too purely innocent a kind for her to require every man to dance attendance on her, yet she is all too aware of the rebel in me.

Sitting thus in the comfortable drawing-room while she, like a good angel, diffuses her charm everywhere, over everyone with whom she comes in contact, over good and evil, I sometimes begin to grow inwardly impatient; I am tempted to rush out from my hiding-place; for though I sit there before everyone's eyes in the drawing-room, I am really sitting in ambush. I am tempted to grasp her hand, to take the whole girl in my arms, to hide her within me in case someone else should take her from me. Or when Edvard and I leave them in the evening, when in taking leave she offers me her hand, when I hold it in mine I find it difficult sometimes to let the bird slip out of my hand. Patience – *quod antea fuit impetus, nunc ratio est* – she must be quite otherwise woven into my web, and then suddenly I let the whole power of love rush forth. We have not spoiled that moment for ourselves with kisses and cuddles, by premature anticipations, for which you can thank me, my Cordelia. I work at developing the contrast, I tense the bow of love to wound the deeper. Like an archer, I slacken the bowstring, tighten it again, listen to its song – it is my martial music – but I do not take aim with it yet, do not even lay the arrow on the string.

When a small number of people often come together in the same room, a kind of tradition soon develops in which each one has his own place, his station; it becomes a picture one can unfold at will, a chart of the terrain. That is also how we unite now to form a picture in the Wahl home. In the evening we drink tea there. Generally the aunt, who until now has been sitting on the sofa, moves over to the little work-table, which place Cordelia in turn vacates. She goes over to the tea-table in front of the sofa, Edvard follows her. I follow the aunt. Edvard tries to be secretive, he wants to whisper, and he usually succeeds so well as to become entirely mute. I make no secrets of my outpourings to the aunt – market prices, a calculation of how many quarts of milk are needed to produce a pound of butter, through the middle-term of cream and the dialectic of the butter-churn; not only do these things form a reality which any young girl can listen to without harm, but, what is far rarer, it is a solid, thorough and edifying conversation, equally improving for mind and heart. I generally sit with my back to the tea-table and the day-dreamings of Edvard and Cordelia. Meanwhile I day-dream with the aunt. And is Nature not great and wise in her productions, is not butter a precious gift, what a glorious result of Nature and art! Certainly the aunt would be unable to hear what passed between Edvard and Cordelia, provided anything passed between them at all; I have promised Edvard that, and I always keep my word. On the other hand, I can easily overhear every word exchanged between them, hear every movement. This is important for me, for one cannot tell how far a desperate man will venture. The most cautious and faint-hearted men sometimes do the most desperate things. Although I thus have nothing at all to do with these two people, I can readily observe from Cordelia that I am constantly an invisible presence between her and Edvard.

Nevertheless it is a peculiar picture we four make. If I were to look for a familiar analogy, I might think of myself as Mephistopheles; but the difficulty is that Edvard is no Faust. If I were to be his Faust, there is the difficulty again that Edvard is no Mephistopheles. Neither am I a Mephistopheles, least of all in Edvard's eyes. He looks on me as his love's good genie, and so he should, for at least he can be sure that no one can watch over his love more solicitously than I. I have promised him to engage the aunt in conversation and I discharge that honourable assignment with all seriousness. The aunt practically vanishes before our own eyes in sheer agricultural economics; we go into the kitchen and cellar, up to the attic, look at the chickens, ducks, and geese, and so on. All this offends Cordelia. What I am really after she cannot of course conceive. I become a riddle to her, but not a riddle that tempts her into wanting to guess, one which irritates her, yes makes her indignant. She has a strong sense that her aunt is almost being made fun of, yet her aunt is a very respectable lady who certainly doesn't deserve that. On the other hand, I do it so well that she is perfectly aware that it would be useless for her to try to put me off. Sometimes I carry things so far that Cordelia secretly has to smile at her aunt. These are necessary exercises. Not that I do this with Cordelia's connivance; far from it, I would never make her smile at her aunt. My expression remains unalterably earnest, but she cannot keep from smiling. It is the first false teaching; we must teach her to smile ironically; but this smile is aimed almost as much at me as at the aunt, for she simply does not know what to think of me.

After all, I might be one of those prematurely old young men; it's possible; there might be another possibility, and a third, and so on. When she has smiled at her aunt she is indignant with herself, I turn around and, without interrupting the conversation with the aunt, look at her quite seriously, then she smiles at me and the situation.

Our relationship is not the tender and loyal embrace of understanding, not attraction, it is the repulsion of misunderstanding. My relationship to her really amounts to nothing at all. It is purely spiritual, which of course to a young girl is nothing at all. The method I am now following has nevertheless extraordinary advantages. Someone who appears as a gallant arouses mistrust and evokes resistance; I am exempt from all that. I am not watched, on the contrary one would rather look upon me as a trustworthy person fit to watch over the young girl. The method has only one fault, it is slow; but for that reason it can be used, and only to advantage, against individuals in whom the prize is the interesting.

What rejuvenating power a young girl has! Not the freshness of the morning air, not the soughing of the wind, not the coolness of the ocean, not the fragrance of wine and its delicious bouquet – nothing else in the world has this rejuvenating power.

Soon I hope to have brought it to the point of her hating me. I have taken on totally the character of a bachelor. I talk of nothing else but sitting at ease, lying comfortably, having a reliable servant, a friend of good standing I can thoroughly trust when on intimate terms. If I can now get the aunt to abandon her agronomic deliberations I shall introduce her to these and so get a more direct opportunity for irony. A bachelor one may laugh at, indeed have some sympathy for, but a young man not without spirit outrages a young girl by such conduct; the significance of her sex, its beauty and poetry, are all destroyed.

So the days pass; I see her, but I do not talk with her. In her presence I talk with the aunt. Occasionally at night it occurs to me to give my love air. Then, wrapped in my cloak, with my hat pulled down over my eyes, I go and stand outside her window. Her bedroom looks out over the yard, but since the house is on a corner it is visible from the street. Sometimes she stands for a moment at the window, or she opens it, looks up at the stars, unobserved by all but the one whom she would least of all think was aware of her. In these night hours I steal about like a wraith, like a wraith I inhabit the place where she lives. I forget everything, have no plans, no calculations, throw reason overboard, expand and strengthen my chest with deep sighs, an exercise I need in order not to suffer from the system which rules my behaviour. Others are virtuous by day and sin at night; by day I am dissimulation, at night pure desire. If she saw me, if she could look into my soul. If!

If this girl would only understand herself, she would have to admit that I am the man for her. She is too intense, too deeply emotional to be happy in marriage, it would not be enough to let her yield to a common seducer; if she yields to me she salvages the interesting from the shipwreck. In relation to me, she must, as the philosophers say with a play on words, *zu Grunde gehen.*

Really, she is tired of listening to Edvard. As always happens, where the interesting is narrowly confined, one discovers all the more. Sometimes she listens to my conversation with the aunt. When I see that, there comes a flash on the far horizon intimating a quite different world, to the surprise of the aunt as well as Cordelia. The aunt sees the lightning but hears nothing, Cordelia hears the voice but sees nothing. The same instant everything is as it was before, the conversation between the aunt and myself proceeds at its uniform pace, like the hooves of post horses in the still of the night; it is accompanied by the samovar's sad singing. At moments like these the atmosphere in the drawing-room can sometimes be unpleasant, especially for Cordelia. She has no one she can talk with or listen to. If she turns to Edvard, she faces the risk of him doing something foolish in his embarrassment. If she turns the other way, to her aunt and me, then the certainty prevailing here, the monotonous hammerblow of our steady conversation, forms the most disagreeable contrast. I can well understand that to Cordelia it must seem that her aunt is bewitched, so completely does she keep in step with my tempo. Nor can she take part in our entertainment; for this is also one of the ways I have used to provoke her, that is, by letting myself treat her altogether as a child. Not that I would permit myself any liberties with her on that account, far from it. I know too well what a disturbing effect such things can have, and it is especially important that her womanliness be able to rise up again pure and lovely. Owing to my intimate relation to the aunt, it is easy for me to treat her like a child who is no judge of the world. Her femininity is not offended by this but merely neutralized; for though it cannot offend her femininity that she knows nothing of market prices, it can irritate her that they should be the most important thing in life. With my powerful support, the aunt outbids herself in this direction. She has become almost fanatical, something she has to thank me for. The only thing about me which she cannot stand is that I am not anything. I have now begun the habit, every time something is said about a vacant position, of saying, 'That's a job for me!', and discussing it very seriously with her. Cordelia always notices the irony, which is exactly as I wish.

Poor Edvard! Too bad he isn't called Fritz. Whenever in my quiet thoughts I dwell on my relation to him, I am reminded of Fritz in *The Bride*. Like his prototype, Edvard is also a corporal in the militia. To tell the truth, Edvard is also distinctly tiresome. He doesn't tackle the matter properly, and he is always too well-dressed and stiff. *Entre nous*, for the sake of our friendship I turn up as casually as possible. Poor Edvard! The only thing that pains me is that he is so infinitely obliged to me that he almost doesn't know how to thank me. To let myself be thanked for it, that's really too much.

*

But why can't you be good children and behave? What have you done all morning except shake my awning, pull at my window mirror and its string, play with the bell-rope from the third floor, push against the windowpanes, in brief, in every possible way proclaim your existence, as if you would beckon me out with you? Yes, the weather is fine, but I have no desire, let me stay at home . . . After all, you boisterous, wanton zephyrs, you happy lads, you can go alone, amuse yourselves with the young maidens as usual. Yes, I know, no one can embrace a maiden as seductively as you; she tries in vain to squirm away from you, she cannot untwine herself from your tangle – and she doesn't want to; for, cool and refreshing, you do not inflame . . . Go your own way, leave me out . . . But then, you say, there's no satisfaction in it, it's not for your own sake . . . very well, then, I'll come with you, but on two conditions. Here is the first. There lives on Kongens Nytorv a young maiden; she is very pretty, but she has the impudence not to want to love me, and what is worse, she loves another, and it has got to the point where they go out walking arm in arm. I know he goes to fetch her at one o'clock. Promise me now that the strongest blowers among you hide somewhere in the vicinity when he comes out of the street door with her. The moment he is about to turn down Store Kongensgade, this detachment rushes forward, in the politest possible manner takes his hat from his head, and carries it at an even speed just two feet in front of him, no faster, for then he might turn back home again. He thinks he is always just on the point of catching it, he doesn't even let go of her arm. In this way you bring them through Store Kongensgade, along the rampart to Nørreport, as far as Høibroplads . . . How long will that take? I'd say about half an hour. At exactly half-past one I approach from Østergade. When the detachment has brought the lovers out into the middle of the Plads, a violent assault is made on them, in which you also whisk off her hat, tangle her curls, carry off her shawl, while all the time his hat floats jubilantly higher and higher into the air; in short, you bring about a confusion, so that not just I but the entire public breaks out into roars of laughter, the dogs begin to bark, and the watchman to toll his bell in the tower. You make her hat fly over to me, so I become the happy individual who restores it to her. – Secondly: the section following me must obey my every signal, keep within the bounds of propriety, offer no affront to any pretty maiden, take no liberty greater than will allow her to preserve her joy during the whole jest, her lips their smile, her eye its tranquillity, and to stay unanxious. If a single one of you dares behave otherwise, your name will be cursed. – And now off with you, to life and joy, to youth and beauty; show me what I have often seen, and never weary of seeing, show me a beautiful young woman, disclose her beauty for me in such a way that she herself becomes even more beautiful; put her to a test that she will enjoy being put to! – I choose Bredgade, but as you know, I have only until half-past one.

There comes a young girl, all smart and starched; today's Sunday, of course . . . Fan her a little, waft her with your coolness, glide in gentle currents about her, embrace her with your touch! I sense the delicate blushing of her cheek, her lips redden, her bosom lifts . . . It's indescribable, isn't it, my girl, it is a blissful delight to inhale these refreshing airs? The little collar bends to and fro and like a leaf. How deeply and soundly she breathes! Her pace slackens, she is almost carried off by the gentle breeze, like a cloud, like a dream . . . Blow a little stronger, in longer puffs! . . . She gathers herself together, the arms drawn closer to her bosom, which she covers more carefully lest a gust of wind prove too forward and steal softly and coolingly beneath the light covering . . . She assumes a more healthy colouring, her cheeks become fuller, her eye clearer, her steps firmer. All vexation makes a person more beautiful. Every young girl should fall in love with the zephyr, for no man knows so well how to enhance her beauty by struggling against her . . . Her body bends a little forward, she looks towards the tips of her toes . . . Stop a little! It is too much, her figure becomes broader, loses its pretty slenderness . . . Cool her a little! . . . It's refreshing, isn't it, my girl, after being warm to feel those invigorating shivers? One could fling open one's arms in gratitude, in joy over existence . . . She turns her side to the breeze . . . Now quick! a powerful gust, so that I can divine the beauty of her contours! . . . A little stronger! to let the draperies close about her more precisely . . . That's too much. Her posture becomes awkward, the light step is disturbed . . . She turns again . . . Blow, now, blow, try her! . . . Enough, too much! One of her curls has fallen . . . will you kindly keep control of yourselves! – Here comes a whole regiment on the march:

Søren Kierkegaard

Die eine ist verliebt gar sehr;
Die andre wäre er gerne.

Yes, it is an undeniably bad appointment in life to walk on one's future brother-in-law's left arm. For a girl this is about the same as a man's being a reserve clerk ... But the clerk can get preferment and has his place in the office, he is called in on exceptional occasions, and that is not the sister-in-law's lot. But her preferment, on the other hand, is not so slow – once she gets promoted and is moved into another office ... Blow now a little more briskly! When one has something firm to hold on fast to, one can offer resistance ... the centre advances vigorously, the wings on either flank were unable to follow ... He stands his ground firmly enough, the wind can't move him, he is too heavy for that – but also too heavy for the wings to be able to lift him from the ground. He thrust himself forward in order to show – that he is a heavy body; but the more unmoved he stands, the more the young girls suffer from it ... My beautiful young ladies, may I not offer a piece of good advice: leave the future husband and brother-in-law out of it, try to walk alone, and you will see, you will find it much more satisfactory ... Blow now a little more softly! ... How they riot in the wind's billows; soon they will be cutting figures in front of each other down the street – can any dance music produce a more frolicsome gaiety? And yet the wind is not exhausting, it gives strength ... Now they sweep along side by side, in full sail down the street – can any waltz carry a young woman away more seductively? And yet the wind does not weary, it supports ... Now they turn round to face the husband and brother-in-law ... Isn't a little opposition pleasant? One likes to struggle to gain possession of what one loves; and one will no doubt succeed, for there is a Providence that comes to the aid of love, that is why the man has the wind in his favour ... Haven't I arranged it well? When you have the wind at your back you can easily steer the loved one past you; but when it blows against you, you are pleasantly excited, then you seek refuge near him, and the wind's breath makes you more wholesome and more tempting, and more seductive, and the wind's breath cools the fruit of your lips which should preferably be enjoyed cold because it is so hot, as champagne is said to be when kept near freezing . . . How they laugh and talk – and the wind carries off the words – is there anything to talk about here now? – and they laugh again and bend before the wind, and hold on to their hats, and watch their feet . . . Stop now, lest the young girls get impatient and angry at us, or afraid of us! – That's it, resolutely and vigorously, the right foot in front of the left . . . How bravely and buoyantly she looks about in the world . . . Do I see correctly? She is hanging on to a man's arm, so she's engaged. Show me, my child, what kind of present you have received on life's Christmas tree? . . . Aha! really it seems to be a very solid fiancé. She's in the first stage of the engagement, then, she loves him – that's certainly possible, and yet her love flutters loosely about him, wide and spacious; she still has the cloak of love which can conceal many . . . Blow a little more! . . . Yes, when one walks so fast it is no wonder the ribbons on her hat stiffen in the wind, that it looks as if they bore this light body like wings – and her love – it follows too, like a fairy veil that the wind plays with. Yes, when you see love like this, it seems so spacious; but when you are about to put it on, when the veil must be resewn into an evening dress – then one won't be able to afford many puffs . . . Lord preserve us! When one has had the courage to take a decisive step for one's entire life, surely one has the heart to walk straight into the wind. Who doubts it? Not I; but temper, temper, my little miss! Time is a hard taskmaster, and the wind is not bad either . . . Tease her a little! . . . What became of the handkerchief? . . . Oh, so you did recover it again . . . There went one of the hat ribbons . . . it is really quite embarrassing for the intended who is present. A girl friend approaches who must be greeted. It is the first time she has seen you since the engagement; of course, showing that you are engaged is the reason you are here on Bredgade, and moreover are thinking of going on to Langelinie. I believe it is the custom for a newly wedded couple to go to Church the first Sunday after the wedding, but engaged couples, on the other hand, go to Langelinie. Yes, an engagement really also has much in common with Langelinie . . . Watch out now! The wind is taking hold of your hat, hold on to it a little, bend your head down . . . What a real shame you got no chance at all to greet your girl friend, not enough calm to greet her with the superior air that an engaged girl ought to assume before the unengaged . . . Blow a little more softly now! . . . Now come the good days . . . how she clings to the beloved; she is just far enough ahead to be able to turn her head back and look up at him, and rejoice in him, her riches, her happiness, her hope, her future . . . Oh my girl, you make too much of him . . . Or won't you allow that he owes it to me and the wind that he looks so vigorous? And don't you yourself owe it to me, and to the soft breezes that now bring you healing and turn pain into oblivion, that you look so full of vitality, so full of longing, so expectant?

> And I will not have a student
> Who lies and reads at night,
> But I will have an officer
> With feathers in his hat.

One can see it in you at once, my girl, there is something in your look . . . No, a student won't do for you . . . But why exactly an officer? A graduate, finished with his studies, couldn't he do just as well? . . . Just now, however, I cannot help you to either an officer or a graduate. But I can help you to some cooling breezes . . . Blow a little harder now! . . . That's right, throw the silk shawl back over your shoulder; walk quite slowly, that should make your cheek a little paler and the eye's lustre more subdued . . . That's it. Yes, a little exercise, especially on a fine day like this, and a little patience, then no doubt you will get your officer. – There's a couple over there who are meant for each other. How measured their steps, what poise their whole appearance presents, built on mutual confidence, what pre-established harmony in all their movements, what assured solidity. Their carriage is not light and graceful, they do not dance with each other, no, there is a durability in them, a forthrightness, which arouses infallible hope and inspires mutual respect. I will wager that their view of life is 'Life is a road'. And they also seem bent on walking with each other arm in arm through life's joys and sorrows. They are so much in harmony that the lady has even given up the privilege of walking on the flagstones . . . But, my dear zephyrs, why are you so busy with that couple? They don't seem worth paying attention to. Is there anything special to take note of? . . . But it is half-past one; off to Høibroplads.

*

One would not think it possible to calculate so accurately a soul's historical development. It shows how healthy Cordelia is. Truly, she is a remarkable girl. Although she is quiet and modest, unde-manding, there is an immense demand lying there unconsciously. – It was obvious to me today when I saw her coming in from the street. It's as though the slight resistance a gust of wind can offer arouses all her powers but without there being any internal conflict. She is not a little insignificant girl who slips between your fingers, so fragile that you are almost afraid she will go to pieces just by looking at her; but neither is she a showy ornamental flower. Like a physician I can therefore observe with pleasure all the symptoms in this case history.

Gradually I am beginning to close in on her in my attack, to go over into a more direct assault. If I were to describe this change on my military map of the family, I would say that I have turned my chair round so that now I am facing her. I have more to do with her, address remarks to her, elicit answers from her. Her soul has passion, intensity, and though not overblown in absurd and vain reflections, it has a hankering for the unusual. My irony at the foolishness of human beings, my scorn of their cowardice, of their lukewarm indolence, fascinate her. She is fond enough of driving the chariot of the sun across the arch of the heavens, of coming too near to the earth and scorching people a bit. She does not trust me, however. Up to now I have obstructed every approach, even in spiritual respects. She must become stronger in herself before I can let her find her repose in me. It may look in flashes as though it were her I would make the confidante in my freemasonry, but it is only in flashes. She herself must be developed inwardly; she must feel her soul's resilience, she must test the world's weight. From her conversation and her eyes I can easily see what progress she is making. Just once I have seen a destructive anger in them. She must owe me nothing, for she must be free; love exists only in freedom, only in freedom are there recreation and everlasting amusement. For although I intend her to fall into my arms through, as it were, natural necessity, and am striving to bring things to the point where she gravitates towards me, it is nevertheless also important that she does not fall as a heavy body, but gravitates as spirit towards spirit. Although she is to belong to me, it mustn't be just in the unaesthetic sense of resting on me like a burden. She must neither be a hanger-on physically speaking nor an obligation morally. Between the two of us must prevail only the proper play of freedom. She must be so light for me that I can take her on my arm.

Cordelia occupies me almost too much. I am losing my equanimity again, not directly in her presence but when alone with her in the strictest sense. I can yearn for her, not to talk with her but just to have her image float by me. When I know she has gone out I can steal after her, not to be seen but to see. The other evening we all left the Baxter house together. Edvard escorted her. In the greatest haste I left them, hurried off to another street where my servant was waiting for me. In a trice I had changed clothes and met her once more without her suspecting. Edvard was silent as usual. Certainly I am in love, but not in the usual sense, and therefore one must also be very careful; there are always dangerous consequences; and after all one is in love only once. Nevertheless, the god of love is blind and if one is clever one can delude him. The trick is to be as receptive in regard to impressions as possible, to know the impression you are making and the impression each girl makes on you. In this way you can even be in love with many at the same time, because with each particular girl you are differently in love. Loving just one is too little; loving all is being superficial; knowing yourself and loving as many as possible, letting your soul hide all the powers of love in itself, so that each gets its particular nourishment while consciousness nevertheless embraces it all – that is enjoyment, that is living.

*

Edvard cannot really complain of me. Certainly, I want Cordelia to burn her fingers on him, so that through him she gets a distaste for run-of-the-mill love and in that way goes beyond her own limitations; but for that very reason it is necessary for Edvard not to be a caricature, for that would not help. Now Edvard is a good match, not just in the bourgeois sense of the word, which means nothing in her eyes (things like that do not cross a seventeen-year-old girl's mind), he has a number of attractive personal qualities which I try to get him to show to best advantage. Like a costumier, like a decorator, I fit him out as well as the house's resources stretch. Indeed, I sometimes hang a little borrowed finery on him. Then when we accompany each other to Cordelia's it is quite strange walking beside him. It is as though he were my brother, my son, and yet he is my friend, my contemporary, my rival. He could ever become a danger to me. So, since he is bound to fall, the higher I can raise him the better; the more consciousness it awakens in Cordelia of what she scorns, the more intense her presentiment of what she desires. I help him to adjust, I commend him, in short I do everything a friend can do for a friend. To set my coldness properly in relief, I behave almost as though I were Edvard's ardent admirer. I portray him as a visionary. Since Edvard has no idea of how to help himself, I have to haul him forward.

Cordelia hates and fears me. What does a young girl fear? Spirit. Why? Because spirit constitutes the negation of her whole feminine existence. Masculine good looks, a charming personality, etc. are good expedients, one can also make conquests with them, but never win a complete victory. Why? Because then one is making war upon a girl on her own ground, and there she is always the stronger. With these methods one can make a girl blush, put her out of countenance, but never call forth that indescribable, captivating anxiety which makes her beauty interesting.

Non formosus erat, sed erat facundus Ulixes,
et tamen aequoreas torsit amore Deas.

Everyone should know his own powers. But something that has often disturbed me is that even those who have natural endowments bungle things so. Really one ought to be able straightaway to see in any young girl who has become the victim of another's, or rather of her own love, in what way she has been deceived. The practised murderer uses a definite stab, and the experienced policeman knows the perpetrator as soon as he sees the wound. But where does one meet such systematic seducers, such psychologists? For most men, seducing a girl means seducing a girl, full stop. And yet there is a whole language concealed in this thought.

As a woman she hates me; as a gifted woman she fears me; as a woman of intelligence she loves me. Now for the first time I have produced this conflict in her soul. My pride, my defiance, my cold scorn, my heartless irony tempt her; not as though she might wish to love me – no, there is certainly no trace of such feelings in her, least of all towards me. She wants to compete with me. What tempts her is the proud independence of people, a freedom like that of the Arabs in the desert. My laughter and oddity neutralize every erotic impulse. She is fairly at ease with me, and so far as there is any reserve, it is more intellectual than feminine. Far from her regarding me as a lover, our relation to each other is that of two able minds. She takes my hand, presses it a little, laughs, is attentive to me in a purely Platonic sense. Then when the ironist and the scoffer have fooled her long enough, I shall follow the directions to be found in an old verse: 'The knight spreads out his cape so red, and begs the beautiful maiden to sit thereon.' However, I do not spread out my cape in order to sit with her on the greensward, but to vanish with her into the air on the wings of thought. Or I do not take her with me but set myself astride a thought, wave farewell, blow a kiss, and vanish from her sight, audible only in the murmur of winged words; not, like Jehovah, in his voice more and more visible, but less and less, because the more I speak, the higher I climb. Then she wants to go with me, off on the wings of bold thoughts. Still, that's only for a single moment; the next instant I am cold and impassive.

There are different kinds of feminine blushes. There is the gross brick-red blush; that's the one romantic writers are always so free with when they have their heroines blush all over. There is the refined blush; it is the blush of the dawn's early light. In a young girl it is above all price. The fleeting blush produced by a happy idea is beautiful in the man, more beautiful in a youth, lovely in a woman. It is a flash of lightning, the sheet lightning of the spirit. It is most beautiful in the young, charming in the girl, because it appears in its virginal state, and for that reason has the bashfulness of surprise. The older one becomes, the less frequently this blush appears.

Sometimes I read something aloud to Cordelia; usually something very inconsequential. Edvard must as usual keep the spotlight. So I have drawn his attention to the fact that a very good way of getting on good terms with a young girl is to lend her books. He has also gained considerably through this, for she is directly beholden to him. It is I who gain most, for I dictate the choice of books and remain remote. This gives me broad scope for my observations. I can give Edvard whatever books I wish, since he is no judge of literature; I can risk what I will, to whatever extreme. Then when I visit her in the evening, I make as if to pick up a book by chance, turn over a few pages, read half-aloud, commend Edvard for his attentiveness. Yesterday evening I wanted to assure myself of her mental resilience by an experiment. I was undecided whether to have Edvard lend her Schiller's poems, so that I could accidentally chance on Thekla's song which I'd then recite, or Bürger's poems. I chose the latter particularly because his 'Lenore', however beautiful, is after all somewhat extravagant. I opened it at 'Lenore', read this poem aloud with all the pathos I could muster. Cordelia was moved, she sewed with a rapid intensity as though it were her Vilhelm had come to fetch. I stopped. The aunt had listened without particular concern. She fears no Vilhelms, living or dead – in any case her German is not all that good – but found herself quite in her element when I showed her the beautifully bound copy and began a conversation about the art of bookbinding. My purpose was to destroy in Cordelia the impression of pathos at the very moment of its arousal. She became a little anxious, but it was clear to me that this anxiety had an uncomfortable effect on her, not a stimulating one.

Today my eyes have rested upon her for the first time. It is said that sleep can make an eyelid so heavy that it closes of its own accord; perhaps this glance of mine has a similar effect. Her eyes close, and yet obscure forces stir within her. She does not see that I am looking at her, she feels it, feels it through her whole body. Her eyes close and it is night, but inside her it is broad daylight.

Edvard must go. He is treading on the boundary. Any moment I can expect him to go to her and make a declaration of love. No one can know that better than I who am his confidant, and who diligently maintains this exaltation so that his effect upon Cordelia can be the greater. To let him confess his love is nevertheless too risky. Although I know quite well she will refuse him, that will not be the end of the affair. He will no doubt take it very much to heart. That might move and touch Cordelia. Although in that event I need not fear the worst, that she should change her mind, still, possibly her self-esteem might suffer through this pure compassion. Should that happen, my plans concerning Edvard are altogether wasted.

My relation to Cordelia is beginning to take a dramatic turn. Something must happen, whatever it may be; I can no longer remain a mere observer without letting the moment slip from me. She has to be surprised, that is necessary; but to surprise her one must be on the alert. What would normally cause surprise might have no effect on her. Really she has to be surprised in such a way that the initial cause of the surprise is, to all intents and purposes, that something quite ordinary happens. It has to appear gradually that there was something surprising in it after all. This is always the law of the interesting, and the latter the law in turn governing all my movements with regard to Cordelia. If only you know how to surprise someone, you have always won the game; for a moment you suspend the energy of the one concerned, make it impossible for her to act, and it makes no difference whether one resorts to the ordinary or the extraordinary. I recall with some satisfaction a foolhardy experiment upon a lady of distinguished family. For some time I had been sneaking around her secretly looking for an interesting form of contact, but in vain; then one day I met her on the street. I was certain she didn't know me or know I belonged here in town. She was walking alone. I slipped past her so that I could meet her face to face. I stepped aside for her; she kept to the flagstones. Just then I cast a sorrowful glance at her, I think I almost had tears in my eyes. I took off my hat. She paused. In an agitated voice and with a dreamy look, I said, 'Do not be angry, gracious lady; the resemblance between you and someone I love with all my soul, but who lives far away from me, is so striking that you must forgive my strange behaviour.' She thought me an extravagant dreamer, and a young girl can well put up with a little extravagance, especially when she also feels her superiority and dares to smile at one. Just so, she smiled, which became her indescribably. With aristocratic condescension she bowed to me, and smiled. She resumed her walk. I walked a few steps by her side. Some days later I met her; I presumed to greet her. She laughed at me ... Patience is a precious virtue, and he who laughs last laughs best.

One could think of several ways of surprising Cordelia. I might try to raise an erotic storm which was capable of tearing up trees by the roots. With its help I could see if I could sweep her off her feet, snatch her from her historic setting, and try in this agitation, by stealthy advances, to arouse her passion. It is not inconceivable that it could be done. A girl with her passion can be made to do anything at all. However, it would be wrong aesthetically. I am not fond of giddiness, and the condition is to be recommended only with girls for whom this is the only way of acquiring a poetic image. Besides, one misses the real enjoyment, for too much confusion is also harmful. On her it will altogether fail of its effect. I might imbibe in a couple of draughts what I could have had the benefit of over a lengthy period, indeed, even worse, what with discretion I might have enjoyed in a way that was fuller and richer. Cordelia is not to be enjoyed in a state of exaltation. It might surprise her in the first instance were I to behave in this way, but she would soon have had enough, precisely because this surprise lay too near her daring soul.

A straightforward engagement is the best of all methods, the most expedient. If she heard me making a prosaic declaration of love, likewise asking her for her hand, she might believe her ears even less than if she listened to my heated eloquence, imbibed my poisoned intoxicant, heard her heart throb at the thought of an abduction.

The damnable thing with an engagement is always the ethical side. The ethical is just as boring in life as it is in learning. What a difference! Beneath the sky of the aesthetic everything is light, pleasant and fleeting; when ethics come along everything becomes hard, angular, an unending ennui. Still, strictly, an engagement has no ethical reality in the way marriage does; its validity is only *consensu gentium*. This ambiguity can be very useful to me. The ethical element in it is just enough for Cordelia at some time to get the impression that she is breaking normal barriers, but not so serious that I will have to fear more critical repercussions. I have always had some respect for the ethical. I have never promised a girl marriage, not even casually; if I seem to be doing so here, it is only a pretence. I shall certainly contrive for her to be the one who breaks off the engagement. My chivalrous pride scorns giving promises. I despise a judge who tricks an offender into a confession with the promise of freedom. A judge like that renounces his own power and ability. Besides, there is the fact that I want nothing in my own practice that is not given freely, in the strictest sense. Let common seducers use such methods! What do they achieve? Anyone unable so to encompass a girl that she loses sight of everything he doesn't want her to see, so to poeticize his way into the girl that it is from her that everything issues, just as he himself would wish it, is and will always be a bungler. I will not envy him his pleasure. A bungler is what such a person is and remains, a seducer, which no one could by any means call me. I am an aesthete, an eroticist, who has grasped the nature and meaning of love, who believes in love and knows it from the ground up. I only reserve to myself the private opinion that no love affair should last more than six months at most, and that every relationship is over as soon as one has tasted the final enjoyment. All this I know; I also know that the highest form of enjoyment conceivable is to be loved, loved more than everything in the world. To poeticize oneself into a girl is an art, to poeticize oneself out of her a masterpiece. Yet the latter depends essentially on the former.

Another method is possible. I could do everything to get her engaged to Edvard. I would become a friend of the family. Edvard would trust me implicitly – after all, I am the one to whom he as good as owes his happiness. In this way I would be better concealed. No, it won't do. She cannot become engaged to Edvard without belittling herself in one way or another. Also, my relationship to her would become more piquant than interesting. The endless prosaicness of an engagement is precisely the sounding-board of the interesting.

Everything is taking on more meaning in the Wahl household. One clearly notes that a hidden life is stirring beneath the daily routine, which must soon proclaim itself in a corresponding revelation. The Wahl household is preparing for an engagement. A mere outside observer might suppose there was to be a match between me and the aunt. What an expansion of agronomic knowledge might such a marriage achieve in a coming generation! I would then become Cordelia's uncle. I am a friend of freedom of thought and no thought is so absurd that I lack courage to grasp hold of it. Cordelia fears a declaration of love from Edvard, Edvard hopes it will decide everything. He may be sure of that. But to spare him the unpleasant consequences of such a step, I shall try to steal a march on him. I am hoping now to be rid of him soon; he really is in my way. I felt it clearly today. Doesn't he look so dreamy and love-drunk that he might suddenly get up, like a somnambulist, and in front of the whole congregation confess his love in such objective terms that he doesn't even approach Cordelia? I looked daggers at him today. I caught Edvard with my eyes, big as he is, as an elephant catches something with its trunk, and threw him over backwards. Although he remained seated in his chair I believe he felt something of the sort in his body.

Cordelia is not showing the same confidence towards me. She always approached me with womanly assurance, now she is a little hesitant. But it is of no great matter and it wouldn't be too difficult for me to bring things back to the old footing. But I won't do that. Just one more exploration and then the engagement. There can be no difficulties there; in her surprise Cordelia will say yes, the aunt a hearty Amen, she will be beside herself with joy over such an agronomic son-in-law. Son-in-law! How everything gets stuck together like pea-straw once one ventures into this area! I don't really become her son-in-law, only her nephew, or rather, God willing, neither.

the 23rd

Today I harvested the fruit of a rumour I had spread, that I was in love with a young girl. With Edvard's help it has also reached the ears of Cordelia. She is curious, she watches me, but she doesn't dare ask; yet it is not unimportant to her to be certain, partly because she finds it unbelievable, partly because she might well see a precedent in this for herself; for if such a cold-blooded scoffer as myself could fall in love, there need be no disgrace in her doing the same. Today I brought up the subject. To tell a story in a way that the point doesn't get lost, I think I'm the man for that, likewise telling it in such a way that the point doesn't emerge too soon. Holding the listeners in suspense, ascertaining through their small incidental movements what they want the outcome to be, putting them off the track in the course of the narration, that's what I like doing; using ambiguities, so the listeners understand one thing by what is being said and then suddenly notice that the words can be understood in another way, that's my *métier*. If what one wants is an opportunity for making certain observations, one should always make a speech. In conversation it is easier for the other party to escape, using questions and answers to hide the impression one's words are producing. In solemn earnest I began my speech to the aunt. 'Am I to impute this to the good-will of my friends or the malice of my enemies, and who hasn't more than enough of both?' Here the aunt made a remark which I helped her to spin out as well as I could so as to keep Cordelia, who was listening, in suspense, a suspense she could not put an end to, since it was the aunt I was talking to and my mood was serious. I continued: 'Or am I to ascribe it to an accident, a rumour's *generatio aequivoca*' (a word Cordelia evidently did not understand – it only confused her, the more so because I put a false emphasis on it and said it with a sly look as if that's where the point lay), 'that I who am used to living a secluded life have become a talking-point by their insisting I am engaged.' Cordelia quite clearly still felt the need of my interpretation. I continued: 'My friends, since it must be considered a piece of good fortune to fall in love' (she started), 'my enemies, since it would be thought quite laughable for this fortune to fall to my lot' (movement in the opposite direction); 'or accident, since there is not the slightest foundation for it; or rumour's *generatio aequivoca*, since the whole thing must have originated in an empty head's thoughtless self-communings.' The aunt with true feminine curiosity lost no time trying to find out who this lady might be with whom it had pleased gossip to betroth me. Every question in this direction was waved aside. On Cordelia the whole story made quite an impression; I rather think Edvard's stock rose a few points.

The decisive moment is nearing. I could address myself to the aunt, asking in writing for Cordelia's hand. This is indeed the customary procedure in affairs of the heart, as if it were more natural for the heart to write than to speak. But it is precisely its philistinism that would decide me to choose it. By doing so I would miss the real surprise, and that I cannot give up. – If I had a friend he might say to me, 'Have you properly considered the very serious step you are taking, a step that is decisive for all the rest of your life, and for another being's happiness?' That's the advantage of having a friend. But I have none. Whether that is an advantage I leave undecided; on the other hand I see it as an absolute advantage to be free of his advice. Otherwise, in the strictest sense of the word, I have certainly thought the whole matter through.

Now there is nothing on my side to prevent the engagement. I proceed accordingly with my courting, though who could see it in me? Soon my humble person will be seen from a higher standpoint. I cease being a person and become – a match; yes, a good match, the aunt will say. It is the aunt I feel most sorry for, for she loves me with so pure and upright an agronomic love, she practically worships me as her ideal.

Now, I have made many declarations of love during my life, yet all my experience is of no help at all here, for this declaration has to be made in a quite special way. What I must mainly bring home to myself is that it is all just a pretence. I have rehearsed several steps to find out which approach would be the best. Making the moment erotic would be dubious, for it might well anticipate what is to come later and ought to develop gradually. Making it very serious is dangerous, for a moment like this is of such great significance for a girl that all her soul may be focused on it, like a dying man's on his last will. Making it easy-going, slapstick, would not be in harmony with the disguise I have used up to now, nor with the new one I plan to construct and adopt. Making it witty and ironical is too risky. If my purpose were the same here as with people in general on such occasions, where the main thing is to coax out the little 'yes', it would be as easy as pie. This is indeed important for me but not absolutely, for although I have now picked out this girl, although I have devoted much attention, indeed all my interest, to her, there are still conditions on which I will not accept her 'yes'. I am not at all interested in possessing the girl in an external sense, but in enjoying her artistically. So the beginning must be as artistic as possible. The beginning must be as vague as possible, an omnipossibility. If she straightaway sees a deceiver in me she misunderstands me, for in an ordinary sense I am no deceiver. If she sees in me a faithful lover she also misunderstands me. The thing is that in this scene her soul must be as little predetermined as possible. In a moment like this a girl's soul is as prophetic as a dying man's. This must be prevented. My lovely Cordelia! I am cheating you out of something beautiful, but it cannot be otherwise, and I shall compensate you as best I can. The whole episode must be kept as inconsequential as possible, so that when she has given her 'yes', she is unable to throw the least light on what may be concealed in this relationship. This infinite possibility is precisely the interesting. If she can predict anything, then I have gone wrong and the whole relationship loses its meaning. It is unthinkable that she should say 'yes' because she loves me, for she does not love me at all. The best thing for me to do is transform the engagement from an action into an event, from something she does into something that happens to her, of which she can say, 'God knows how it really came about.'

the 31st

Today I have written a love-letter for a third party. This is a constant source of pleasure. In the first place, it is always extremely interesting to enter so vividly into the situation, yet in all possible comfort. I have my pipe filled, hear about the relationship, the letters from the parties in question are produced. It is a matter of constant interest to me how a young girl writes. The man sits there now, infatuated as a rat, reading her letters aloud and interrupted by my laconic remarks: she writes well, she has feeling, taste, caution, she has certainly been in love before, etc. Secondly, it is a good deed. I am helping to bring a young couple together. For every happy couple, I select one victim for myself. I make two people happy, just one unhappy at most. I am honest and reliable, and have never deceived anyone who has confided in me. There is always a little fun among the leavings, after all that's just legal fees. And why do I enjoy this trust? Because I know Latin and attend to my studies, and because I always keep my little affairs to myself. And don't I deserve this confidence? After all, I never abuse it.

August 2nd

The moment had arrived. I caught a glimpse of the aunt on the street, so I knew she was not at home. Edvard was at the tolbooth. Accordingly there was every likelihood that Cordelia was at home alone. And so it proved. She sat at the work-table busy with a piece of sewing. Very rarely have I visited the family before dinner, so she was a little disturbed at seeing me. The situation came close to becoming too emotional. She wouldn't have been to blame for that, for she controlled herself quite easily, but I myself; for in spite of my armour she made an unusually strong impression upon me. How charming she was in a blue-striped, simple calico house-dress, with a fresh-plucked rose on her bosom – a fresh-plucked rose! no, the girl herself was like a freshly plucked flower, so fresh she was, newly arrived; and who knows where a young girl spends the night? In the land of illusions, I believe, but every morning she returns, hence her youthful freshness. She looked so young and yet full-grown, as if Nature, like a tender and copious mother, had just at that moment let her out of her hand. It was almost as though I were witness to that farewell scene; I saw how that loving mother embraced her once more in farewell, I heard her say, 'Go out now into the world, my child, I have done everything I can for you; take this kiss as a seal on your lips, it is a seal that guards the sanctuary; no one can break it unless you yourself wish it so, but when the right one comes, you will know him.' And she pressed a kiss on her lips, a kiss which did not, as a human kiss, take something but was like a divine kiss that gives everything, that gives the girl the power of the kiss. Marvellous Nature, how profound and mysterious you are! You give to the man the word, and to the girl you give the eloquence of the kiss! This kiss was upon her lips, and the farewell blessing on her forehead, and the joyous salutation in her eyes; therefore she looked at once so much at home, for she was after all the child of the house, but at the same time so much a stranger, for she did not know the world but only her fond mother who watched invisibly over her. She was really delightful, young as a child and yet adorned with that noble maidenly dignity that inspires respect. – However, I was quickly dispassionate again and solemnly unemotional, as is fitting when one wants to make something significant occur in a way that makes it seem of no consequence. After some general remarks, I moved a little nearer to her, and then got on with my proposal. A person who speaks like a book is exceedingly boring to listen to; sometimes, however, it is not inappropriate to talk in that way. For a book has the remarkable property that it can be interpreted any way you wish. If one talks like a book one's conversation acquires this property too. I kept quite soberly to the usual formulas. She was surprised, as I'd expected; that can't be denied. To describe to myself how she looked is difficult. She seemed multifaceted; yes just about like the still to be published but announced commentary to my book, a commentary capable of any interpretation. One word and she would have laughed at me; another and she would have been moved; still another and she would have shunned me; but no such word came to my lips. I remained solemnly unemotional and kept to the ritual. 'She had known me for such a short time', dear God, it's only on the strait path of engagement one meets such difficulties, not on the primrose path of love.

Strangely enough, when pondering the matter the previous days, I was rather hasty and quite sure that in the moment of surprise she would say yes. One sees what all the preparation was good for, for that's not how things turned out; she said neither yes nor no but referred me to the aunt. I should have foreseen that. But really I have luck on my side all the same, for this was an even better outcome.

The aunt gives her consent. And I hadn't entertained the slightest doubt about that either. Cordelia follows her advice. As for my engagement, I do not brag that it is poetic, it is extremely philistine and petty bourgeois in every way. The girl does not know whether she should say yes or no, the aunt says yes, the girl too says yes, I take the girl, she takes me – and now the story begins.

the 3rd

So I'm engaged; so is Cordelia, and I suppose that's just about all she knows of the matter. If she had a friend she could speak frankly with, she'd no doubt say, 'What it all means I've really no idea. Something about him attracts me, but what it is I can't make out; he has a strange power over me; but love him, no, I don't, and perhaps never will; on the other hand I should certainly be able to endure living with him and can therefore be very happy with him, for surely he doesn't ask too much if only one puts up with him.' My dear Cordelia! perhaps he demands more, and in return less endurance. – Of all ridiculous things, engagement must be the most ridiculous of all. In marriage there's at least meaning, even though that meaning doesn't suit me. An engagement is a purely human invention and reflects no credit at all on its inventor. It is neither one thing nor the other, and has as much to do with love as the strip hanging down the beadle's back has with a professor's gown. I am now a member of this honourable company. That is not without significance, for, as Trop says, it is only by being an artist that one acquires the right to judge other artists. And is not a fiancé also a Dyrehaug's artist?

Edvard is beside himself with indignation. He is letting his beard grow and has hung up his dark suit, which says a lot. He wants to speak with Cordelia, wants to describe my deviousness to her. That will be a scandalous scene, Edvard unshaven, negligently dressed, shouting at Cordelia. So long as he doesn't cut me out with his long beard. I try in vain to bring him to reason; I explain that it is the aunt who has brought about the match, that maybe Cordelia still harbours feelings for him, that I shall be willing to withdraw if he can win her. He hesitates a moment, wonders whether he shouldn't let his beard jut out in some new fashion, buy a new dark suit; the next moment he is abusing me. I do everything to keep up appearances with him. However angry he is with me, I am certain he will take no step without consulting me; he doesn't forget the advantages of having me as mentor. And why should I take from him his last hope, why break with him? He is a good man; who knows what the future may bring?

What I must do now is, on the one hand, prepare everything for the breaking-off of the engagement, so as to ensure a more beautiful and more significant relationship with Cordelia; and on the other, make use of the time as well as I can to delight in all the lovableness that Nature has so abundantly equipped her with, delight in it, though within the limits and with the circumspection that prevents any anticipation. Then when I have brought it to the point of her learning what it is to love, and to love me, the engagement breaks like an imperfect mould and she is mine. Others get engaged when they reach this point, and have good prospects of a boring marriage for all eternity. That's their business.

Everything is still *status quo*. But a fiancé could scarcely be more fortunate than I, no miser who has found a gold piece could be more blissful. I am intoxicated with the thought that she is in my power. A pure, innocent femininity, as translucent yet as profound as the ocean, with no suspicion what love is! Now she will learn what kind of power love is. Like a king's daughter who is raised from the dust to the throne of her forefathers, she shall now be installed in the kingdom that is her own. And it is through me it will happen; she learns to love me in learning to love; in extending her rule, the paradigm gradually increases, and that is me. In feeling her whole significance to lie in love, she expends that significance upon me, she loves me doubly. The thought of my joy is so overwhelming that I almost take leave of my senses.

Her soul is not dissipated or slackened with love's indeterminate stirrings, something that prevents many girls from ever learning to love categorically, energetically, totally. They have in their consciousness an indefinite, hazy picture that is meant to be the ideal against which the actual object is to be tested. From such half-measures emerges something which can help one along one's Christian way through the world. – As love now awakens in her soul, I look through it, heed it as it emerges from her with all love's voices. I ascertain what shape it has taken in her and myself conform to it; and as I am already an immediate part of the story, the love that courses through her heart, so I come to meet her once more, from outside, as deceptively as possible. After all, a girl loves only once.

I am now in lawful possession of Cordelia, I have the aunt's consent and blessing, the congratulations of friends and relations. That should do it. Now all the hardships of war are over, the blessings of peace begin. What tomfoolery! As if the aunt's blessing and the friends' congratulations could in any real sense put me in possession of Cordelia; as if love made such a contrast between wartime and peace, and did not, as long as it lasts, proclaim itself rather in conflict, however different the weapons. The difference is really whether it is fought *cominus* or *eminus*. The more the conflict in a love affair has been *eminus*, the more it is to be deplored, for in that case the less significant the hand-to-hand combat. To the latter belong the handclasp and the touching of the foot, both of which, as we know, were as warmly recommended by Ovid as most jealously disparaged, to say nothing of a kiss, an embrace. Someone fighting *eminus* has usually only his eye to rely on, yet if he is an artist he will be able to employ this weapon with such virtuosity that he accomplishes almost the same. He will be able to let his eye rest upon a girl with a desultory tenderness that affects her in the same way as if he had accidentally touched her; he will be able to hold her as firmly with his eye as if he held her in his embrace. It is always a mistake, however, or a misfortune, to fight *eminus* for too long, for a fight of that kind is not the enjoyment itself, always just an indication. It is only when one fights *cominus* that everything assumes its true importance. When love stops fighting it has come to an end. I have as good as not fought *eminus* at all, and am now therefore not at the end but the beginning; I am bringing out my weapons. True, I do possess her in a legal and petty bourgeois sense, but to me that means nothing at all; I have far purer ideas. True, she is indeed engaged to me, but to infer from this that she loved me would be a deception, for she isn't in love at all. I have lawful possession of her, yet I do not possess her as I might very well possess a girl without having lawful possession.

Auf heimlich erröthender Wange
Leuchtet des Herzens Glühen.

She is sitting on the sofa by the tea-table, I in a chair by her side. This positioning has confidentiality but also an exclusiveness that makes for distance. So very much always depends on the positions; that is, for one who has an eye for it. Love has many positionings; this is the first. How royally Nature has endowed this girl, her pure soft contours, her deep feminine innocence, her clear eyes – everything intoxicates me. – I have paid her my respects. She came towards me cheerfully as usual, though a little embarrassed, a little uncertain; the engagement ought after all to change our relationship, but she doesn't know how. She took my hand, but not with the usual smile. I returned the greeting with a slight, almost imperceptible pressure on the hand; I was gentle and friendly though without being amorous. – She is sitting on the sofa by the tea-table, I in a chair by her side. A beautifying solemnity suffuses the situation, a soft morning radiance. She is silent; nothing disturbs the stillness. My eye glides softly over her, not with desire, that indeed would be shameless. A delicate, momentary blush fleets over her, like a cloud over a meadow, rising and receding. What does this blush mean? Is it love? Is it longing, hope, fear? Because the heart's colour is red? Not at all. She is surprised, she marvels – not at me, that would be too little to offer her; she marvels not at herself but inside herself, she is transformed within. This moment demands stillness, so no reflection must disturb it, no noise of passion interrupt it. It is as though I were not present, and yet my presence is precisely what furnishes the condition for this contemplative wonder of hers. My being is in harmony with hers. In a condition like this, a young girl is to be worshipped and adored, like some deities, in silence.

It is fortunate that I have my uncle's house. If I wanted to give a young man a distaste for tobacco, I would take him to one or other smoking-room at the Regent's. If I want to give a young girl a distaste for being engaged, I need only introduce her here. Just as in the tailors' guildhall one looks only for tailors, so one looks here only for engaged couples. It is a frightful company to fall into and I cannot blame Cordelia for becoming impatient. When we are assembled *en masse* I think we can muster ten couples, besides the supplementary battalions that come to the capital on big festive occasions. Then we betrothed could really enjoy the pleasures of betrothal. I meet with Cordelia at the alarm-post to give her a distaste for these infatuated clinches, these journeyman's bunglings. All evening one constantly hears a sound as of someone going round with a fly-swatter – it is the kiss of the lovers. There is an amiable lack of constraint in this house, one doesn't seek out the dark corners; no! one sits around a big round table. I make as if to submit Cordelia to the same treatment. For that I have to do violence to myself. It would be really outrageous to let myself insult her profound femininity in that manner. I would reproach myself for this more than for deceiving her. In general, I can guarantee a perfect treatment, aesthetically, of any girl who puts her trust in me: except that it ends in her being deceived; but that is consistent with my aesthetics, for either the girl deceives the man or the man deceives the girl. It would be quite interesting if one could get some literary hack to find out in fairy stories, sagas, ballads and mythologies whether a girl is more frequently unfaithful than a man.

I do not regret the time that Cordelia costs me, although it is considerable. Every meeting requires, often, long preparation. With her I am witnessing the birth of her love. I am myself as though present invisibly when sitting visibly by her side. As when a dance which should really be danced by two is only danced by one, that's how my relation is to her. For I am the other dancer, but invisible. She moves as though in a dream, yet she is dancing with another, and this other, it is I who inasmuch as I am visibly present am yet invisible, inasmuch as I am invisibly present am yet visible. The movements require another person: she bows to him, she gives him her hand, she draws back, she draws near him again. I take her hand, I complete her thought, which is nevertheless complete in itself. She moves in the melody of her own soul, I am only the occasion for her moving. I am not amorous, that would only awaken her; I am flexible, yielding, impersonal, almost like a mood.

What as a rule do engaged couples talk about? As far as I know, they are busily occupied in getting themselves mutually enmeshed in the tiresome connections of the respective families. No wonder the erotic disappears. Unless one can make the erotic the absolute in comparison with which all other history vanishes, one should never get mixed up with loving, even if one marries ten times. If I have an aunt called Mariane, an uncle called Christopher, a father who is a major, etc., all such public knowledge is irrelevant to the mysteries of love. Yes, even one's own past life is nothing. Usually a young girl hasn't so much to report in this respect; if she does, listening to her may be worth while, but not, as a rule, loving. Personally, I am not looking for histories; I have more than enough of them. I am looking for immediacy. That the individuals first exist for one another in its instant is the eternal element in love.

A little trust must be awoken in her, or rather, a doubt must be removed. I am not exactly one of those loving people for whom it is out of respect that they love one another, marry one another, beget children with one another; yet I am well aware that love, especially when passion is not yet aroused, requires of the one concerned that he should not offend aesthetically against morality. In this regard love has its own dialectic. Thus, while from the point of view of morality my relation to Edvard is far more reprehensible than my behaviour to the aunt, it would be much easier for me to justify the former to Cordelia than the latter. Although she hasn't said anything, I have nevertheless found it best to explain to her the necessity of my acting in this way. The caution I have used flatters her pride, the secrecy with which I have handled everything fascinates her. Certainly, it might seem that I have already betrayed too much erotic refinement here, that I shall contradict myself if I must later convey the idea that I have never loved before, but that doesn't matter. I am not afraid of contradicting myself so long as she doesn't notice it and I achieve what I want. Let scholarly disputants take pride in avoiding all contradiction; a young girl's life is too rich for there not to be contradictions in it and so makes contradiction necessary.

She is proud and also has no real conception of the erotic. While she now defers to me, to some extent, in spiritual respects, it is conceivable that when the erotic begins to assert itself, she may take it into her head to turn her pride against me. As far as I can see, she is confused about what it really means to be a woman. That is why it was easy to arouse her pride against Edvard. This pride was quite eccentric, however, because she had no conception of love. If she acquires it, then she acquires her true pride. But a residue of the eccentric pride could remain. Conceivably she might then turn against me. Although she will not regret having agreed to the engagement, nevertheless it will be clear to her that I made a rather good bargain; she will realize that the beginning was improperly effected on her part. If this should dawn on her, she will venture to defy me. That's how it should be. I shall know then for certain how deeply moved she is.

*

Sure enough. Already, far down the street, I see this delightful little curly head stretching out of the window as far as it can. This is the third day I've noticed it ... A young girl certainly doesn't stand at the window for nothing, she presumably has her own good reasons ... But for heaven's sake, I beg you, don't stretch out so far; I bet you are standing on the stretcher of the chair, I can tell from the posture. Think how terrible it would be to fall on your head – not on me, for I'm staying out of this affair for the time being, but on him, him, yes, after all there must be a him ... No, what do I see over there? If it isn't my friend licenciate Hansen walking down the middle of the street. There's something unusual in his appearance, the method of transportation is unaccustomed; if I'm right he approaches on the wings of longing. Can it be that he has the run of this house? And without my knowledge? ... My pretty miss, you have disappeared; I imagine you have gone down to open the door for his reception ... You might as well come back, he is not coming to your house at all ... How do I know that? I can assure you ... he said so himself. If the wagon that went past hadn't been so noisy you could have heard it yourself. I said to him, quite casually you understand, 'Are you going in here?' To which he replied no, in so many words ... You might as well say goodbye, for now the licenciate and I are going for a walk. He is embarrassed, and embarrassed people tend to be talkative. So I shall talk to him about the living he is applying for ... goodbye, my pretty miss, we are going now to the tolbooth. When we get there I shall say to him, 'Well, damned if you haven't taken me out of my way, I should be up on Vestergade.' – Look, now we're here again ... what faithfulness, she's still standing at the window. A girl like that should make a man happy ... And why then, you ask, do I do all this? Because I'm a mean-hearted man who delights in teasing others? Not at all. I do it out of concern for you, my amiable miss. In the first place, you have waited for the licenciate, yearned for him, so now when he arrives he is doubly handsome. Secondly, when he comes in the door now, he says, 'Heavens! We were nearly caught, that damned man was standing there at the door just as I was going to visit you. But I was smart, I got him involved in a long chat about the call I'm applying for, and walked him up and down and in the end as far as the tolbooth; I give you my word, he noticed nothing.' And so? Well, you are even more fond of the licenciate than before, you always thought he had an excellent mind, but that he was smart . . . well, now you can see for yourself. And you have me to thank for that. – But something occurs to me. Your engagement can't have been announced, otherwise I'd know about it. The girl is delicious and a joy to behold, but she is young. Perhaps her insight is not yet mature. Isn't it conceivable that she might go and take a very serious step thoughtlessly? It must be prevented, I must speak to her. I owe her that, for she is certainly a very amiable girl. I owe it to the licenciate, for he is my friend. And as for that, I owe it to her because she is my friend's intended. I owe it to her family, for it is no doubt a very respectable one. I owe it to the whole human race, for it is a good deed. The whole human race! Great thought, inspiring achievement, to act in the name of the whole human race, to possess such general power of attorney! – But now for Cordelia. I can always make use of mood, and the girl's beautiful yearning has really affected me.

So now begins the first war with Cordelia, in which I take to my heels and so teach her to triumph in her pursuit of me. I keep on retreating, and in this backward movement I teach her to recognize in me all the powers of love, its uneasy thoughts, its passion, what longing is, and hope and restless expectation. By my putting on this show for her, all this develops correspondingly in her. It is a triumphal procession that I lead her into, and I am as much the dithyrambic singer of paeans in praise of her victory as I am the one who shows the way. She will gain the courage to believe in love, to believe it is an eternal power, when she sees its dominion over me, sees my movements. She will believe me, partly because I count on my art, partly because at the bottom of what I do there is truth. If it were not so, she would not believe me. With every movement of mine she becomes stronger and stronger; love awakens in her soul, she is initiated into the meaning of her womanhood. – Up to now, in the petty-bourgeois sense, I have not

77

proposed to her personally; I do it now, I set her free; only thus will I love her. She must never suspect that she owes it to me, for then she loses her self-confidence. It is when she feels free, so free that she is almost tempted to break with me, that the second conflict begins. She has power and passion now, and the conflict has importance for me whatever the immediate consequences. Suppose her pride makes her giddy, suppose she breaks with me; well, then, she has her freedom, but she is going to belong to me nevertheless. Of course, it is tomfoolery that the engagement should bind her; I want only to own her in her freedom. Let her leave me, the second conflict will begin all the same, and in the second conflict I shall triumph as surely as it was an illusion that she triumphed in the first. The greater the power in her, the more there is in it for me. The first war is the war of liberation, it is a game; the second is a war of conquest, it is a matter of life and death.

Do I love Cordelia? Yes! Genuinely? Yes! Faithfully? Yes! – in an aesthetic sense, and surely even that means something. What good would it do this girl if she fell into the hands of a numbskull of a faithful husband? What would become of her? Nothing. It is said that loving such a girl takes rather more than honesty. I have that more – it is duplicity. And still I love her faithfully. Sternly and temperately I keep myself in check, so that everything there is in her, all her divinely rich nature, is allowed to unfold. I am one of the few that can do that, she one of the few who are fit for it; are we then not suited to each other?

Is it wrong of me, instead of looking at the priest, to fix my eye on the beautiful embroidered handkerchief you hold in your hand? Is it wrong of you to hold it that way? ... It has a name in the corner ... Charlotte Hahn, is that what you are called? It is so seductive to learn a lady's name in such an accidental manner. It is as if there were a willing spirit who mysteriously made me acquainted with you ... Or is it not an accident that the handkerchief was folded just right for me to see your name? ... You are troubled, you dry a tear from your eye, the handkerchief hangs down loosely again . . . It is obvious to you that I am looking at you, not at the preacher. You look at the handkerchief, you realize it has betrayed your name . . . It is really a very innocent matter: it is easy to get to know a girl's name . . . Why take it out on the handkerchief, why should it be crumpled up? Why be angry with it? Why be angry with me? Listen to what the priest says: 'No one should lead a man into temptation; even one who does so without knowing has a responsibility, he too owes a debt to the other, a debt he can discharge only by greater good-will' . . . Now he has said Amen. Outside the church door there's nothing to stop the handkerchief fluttering loosely in the wind . . . or have you become afraid of me? What have I done? . . . Have I done more than you can forgive, than you dare remember – in order to forgive?

A double movement will be needed for Cordelia. If all I do is constantly withdraw before her superior strength, the erotic in her might well become too diffuse and relaxed for the deeper womanliness to hypostatize itself. Then, when the second conflict begins, she would be unable to offer resistance. She may certainly sleep her way to victory, indeed that's what she must do; on the other hand she must be constantly awakened. So when it seems to her for a moment as though her victory were wrested from her again, she must learn to want to keep hold of it. In this wrestling her womanliness is matured. I could either use conversation to inflame and letters to cool, or conversely. The latter alternative is in every way preferable. I can then enjoy her most extreme moments. When she has received an epistle, when its sweet poison has been absorbed into her blood, a word is enough to make the love erupt. The next moment my irony and iciness put her in doubt, yet not so much that she cannot constantly feel her victory, feel it increased on receipt of the next epistle. Nor is irony so easy to deploy in a letter, without running the risk of her not understanding it. It is only in small glimpses that ardour can be deployed in conversation. My personal presence will prevent the ecstasy. When I am there only in a letter, she can easily stand up to me, she to some extent confuses me with a universal being who lives in her love. Also, in a letter it is easier to let oneself go; in a letter I can very well throw myself at her feet, etc., something that would very likely look nonsensical were I actually to do it, and the illusion would be destroyed. The contradiction in these movements will evoke and develop, strengthen and consolidate the love in her, in a word, tempt it. –

Yet these letters mustn't assume too soon a strongly erotic tone. To begin with it is best they bear a more universal imprint, contain a hint or two, remove a doubt or two. There can also be the occasional suggestion of the advantage an engagement has, inasmuch as it enables one to keep people away through mystification. What imperfections it otherwise has there will be no lack of opportunity to observe. I can keep up, in my uncle's house, the continual accompaniment of a caricature. The eroticism of the heart she cannot evoke without my help. When I deny it and let this caricature torment her, she will become wearied of being engaged soon enough, yet without really being able to say that it is I who have wearied her of it.

A little epistle today will give her a hint of the taste of her soul by describing the state of my own. That's the right method. And method is what I have; for that I can thank you dear young girls whom I have loved before. I owe it to you that my soul is so attuned that I can be whatever I wish to Cordelia. I remember you gratefully, the honour is yours; I shall always admit that a young girl is a born teacher from whom it is always possible to learn, if nothing else, how to deceive her – for that's something best learnt from the girls themselves. No matter how old I become, I shall never forget that a man is only finished when he is too old to learn anything from a young girl.

My Cordelia!

You say that you hadn't imagined me like this, but nor did I imagine I could be like this. Isn't the change rather in you? Might it not really be that it wasn't I that had changed but the eye with which you see me. It is in me because I love you, in you because it is you that I love. With the cold, calm light of reason I surveyed everything, proud and unmoved, nothing made me afraid, nothing took me by surprise, even if the spirit had knocked at my door I'd have calmly taken up the candelabrum in order to open it. But there, it wasn't ghosts I opened the door to, not pale, powerless figures, it was you, my Cordelia, it was life and youth and beauty that came to meet me. My arm trembles, I cannot hold the light steady, I back away from you, unable, however, to take my eyes off you, unable not to wish I could hold the light still. Yes, I am changed, but to what, in what way, in what does this change consist? I don't know, I don't know what further description to add, what richer predicate to use than this, when infinitely enigmatically I say of myself: I am changed.

Your Johannes

My Cordelia!

Love loves secrecy – an engagement is a revelation; it loves silence – an engagement is a public announcement; it loves whispering – an engagement is a loud-voiced proclamation. Yet with my Cordelia's art, an engagement will be just what is needed for deceiving the foe. On a dark night there is nothing more dangerous for other ships than to hang out a lamp more deceptive than the darkness.

Your Johannes

She's sitting on the sofa by the tea-table, I sit by her side; she's holding my arm, her head rests on my shoulder, weighed down by many thoughts. She is so near, yet so distant. She gives herself up to me, yet does not belong to me. There is still resistance, but not consciously so; it is the usual resistance of womanhood, for woman's nature is submission in the form of resistance. – She's sitting on the sofa by the tea-table, I sit by her side. Her heart is throbbing but without passion, her bosom moves but not in disquiet, at times her colouring changes but in easy transitions. Is this love? Not at all. She listens, she understands. She heeds the winged word, she understands it; she listens to what another says, she understands it as though it were something she herself had said; she heeds the voice of another as it echoes inside her; she understands this echo as though it were her own voice issuing forth both to her and to another.

What am I doing? Am I deluding her? Not at all, that would be no use. Am I stealing her heart? Not at all, I would sooner make sure that the girl I loved kept her heart. Then what am I doing? I am fashioning for myself a heart in the likeness of her own. An artist paints his beloved, that's his pleasure; a sculptor forms her. That's what I am doing too, but in a spiritual sense. She doesn't know I possess this picture, and that is really where my duplicity lies. I have got hold of it secretly, and in that sense I have stolen her heart, as Rebecca is said to have stolen Laban's heart when she deviously defrauded him of his household gods.

The setting and frame have, after all, a great influence on one, are part of what is stamped most firmly and deeply on the memory, or rather on one's whole soul, and are therefore never forgotten. However old I get, I will never be able to think of Cordelia in other surroundings than this little room. When I come to visit her, the maid generally lets me in from the hall; Cordelia comes in from her room and she opens her door just as I open the door to enter the drawing-room, so our eyes meet straightaway at the doorway. The drawing-room is small, comfortable, hardly more than a closet. Although I have seen it now from many different angles, what I'm most fond of is the view from the sofa. She sits there by my side; in front of me stands a round tea-table, over which a tablecloth is draped in rich folds. On the table stands a lamp, shaped like a flower, which shoots up, vigorous and full-bodied, to bear its crown, over which in turn a delicately cut paper shade hangs down, so lightly that it can never stay still. The lamp's shape reminds me of oriental nature, the movements of the shade of the gentle breezes in those parts. The floor is covered with a carpet woven from some kind of osier, a piece of work that immediately betrays its foreign origin. At times I let the lamp become the motif for my landscape. I'm sitting there, with her outstretched on the ground, under the lamp's flower. At other times I let the osier rug evoke the idea of a ship, of an officer's cabin – we are sailing out into the middle of the great ocean. When we sit far away from the window, we are gazing straight into heaven's vast horizon. This too adds to the illusion. Then when I sit by her side, I let these things appear like a picture fleeting swiftly over reality, as death walks over one's grave. The setting is always of great importance, especially for memory's sake. Every erotic relationship should be lived in such a way that one can easily conjure up an image which possesses all of its beauty. To succeed, in this, one must pay particular attention to the setting. If one doesn't find the setting one wants, it has to be come by. In the case of Cordelia and her love the setting fits perfectly. What a different picture comes to mind when I think of my little Emilie, and yet again, how suitable the setting! I can't imagine her except in the little garden room, or rather it is only there that I want to remember her. The doors stood open, a small garden in front of the house obstructed the view, forcing the eye to stop there, to pause before the boldly trodden highway which disappeared into the distance. Emilie was delightful, but more insignificant than Cordelia. The setting was also made for that. The eye remained earthbound, it did not rush boldly and impatiently on, it rested on this little foreground; as for the highway, even though it lost itself romantically in the distance, its effect was more to make the eye traverse the stretches that lay before one, and turn back to this garden in order to traverse the same distance once again. The apartment was on earth. Cordelia's setting must have no foreground, but the infinite boldness of the horizon. She must not be on earth, but float, not walk but fly, not to and fro, but everlastingly onward.

When one gets engaged, one is initiated immediately into all of engagement's humbug. Some days ago licenciate Hansen turned up with the attractive young girl he has become engaged to. He confided to me that she was a delight, I knew that already; he confided to me that she was very young, I knew that too; finally he confided to me that it was for that very reason he had chosen her, to fashion her into the ideal which had always floated before his eyes. Heavens above! such a silly licenciate – and a healthy, blooming, joyous girl. Now, I am a fairly old practitioner, yet I never draw near a young girl other than as to Nature's *venerabile* and learn first from her. In so far as I may then have any educative influence on her, it is by teaching her again and again what I have learned from her.

Her soul must be moved in all possible directions, not piecemeal, however, and in sudden gusts, but totally. She must discover the infinite, and find out that this is what comes most naturally to a human being. She must discover this not by way of thought – for her that is a detour – but in imagination, which is the real means of communication between her and me; for what in man is part, in the woman is the whole. Not for her to work her way towards the infinite along the laborious path of thought, for the woman is not born to toil; it is along the gentle path of the heart and imagination that she must grasp it. For a young girl, the infinite is as natural as the idea that all love must be happy. Everywhere, in whichever direction she turns, a young girl is surrounded by infinitude; the transition is a leap, but bear in mind that it is a womanly leap, not a manly one. Why are men generally so clumsy? When they are about to leap they first take a little run-up, make lengthy preparations, measure the distance with the eye, take several running starts, then get afraid and turn back again. Finally they leap and don't make it. A young girl leaps in a different way. In mountain regions one often comes across two towering peaks. A yawning chasm separates them, terrible to gaze down into. No man dares this leap. A young girl, however, so the local inhabitants say, has dared it, and it is called the Maiden's Leap. I am prepared to believe it, as I believe everything remarkable about a young girl, and for me it is an intoxicant to hear the simple inhabitants speaking of it. I believe everything, believe the miraculous, am amazed at it simply in order to believe; just as the only thing that has astonished me in the world is a young girl, the first; and it will be the last. And yet a leap like that for a young girl is only a jump, while a man's leap will always be ridiculous because, however long his stride, his exertion is as nothing compared with the distance between the peaks, though it offers a kind of yardstick. But who could be fool enough to imagine a young girl taking a run-up? Certainly one can imagine her running, but then the running is itself a game, an enjoyment, an unfolding of grace, while the idea of a run-up separates what in a woman go together. For a run-up has the dialectical in it, and that is contrary to woman's nature. And now the leap; who dares be so ungracious as to separate here what go together? Her leap is an effortless floating. And when she reaches the other side, she stands there again, not exhausted by exertion, but more than usually beautiful, fuller in her soul, she throws a kiss over to us who stand on this side. Young, new-born, like a flower sprung up from the roots of the mountain, she swings out over the abyss, so that we almost turn giddy. – What she must learn is to make all the movements of infinitude, to rock to and fro, to lull herself into moods, to exchange poesy and reality, truth and romance, to be tossed about in infinity. Then when she is familiar with this tumult, I put the erotic in place, and she becomes what I wish and desire. Then my good turn is done, my labour; I take in all my sails, I sit by her side, it is under her sail we journey on. And truly, when this girl is first erotically intoxicated, I shall have enough to do in sitting at the helm to moderate the speed, so that nothing comes too early, nor in an unpleasing manner. Once in a while I puncture a little hole in the sail, and the next moment we are foaming along once more.

In my uncle's house Cordelia becomes more and more indignant. Several times she has proposed that we do not go there again. It's no use, I always know how to hit upon subterfuges. Last night when we left she pressed my hand with unusual passion. She had presumably really felt pained by being there, and no wonder. If I didn't always derive amusement from observing the unnatural products of their artifice I couldn't possibly endure it. This morning I received a letter from her in which, with more wit than I had given her credit for, herewith, she ridicules engagements. I kissed the letter; it is the most precious I have received from her. Just so, my Cordelia! That's how I want it.

*

By a remarkable coincidence there are two confectioners on Østergade opposite each other. On the first floor on the left lives a little young lady, or lady's maid. She usually hides behind a venetian blind which covers the windowpane where she sits. The blind is made of very thin material, and anyone who knows the girl or has seen her often will easily be able, if he has good eyes, to make out every feature; while to anyone who doesn't know her and does not have good eyes, she appears as a dark shadow. The latter is to some extent the case with me, the former that of a young officer who can be seen in the offing every day precisely at noon and who looks up at this blind. Really what first drew my attention to this beautiful telegraphic situation was the fact that there are no blinds on the remaining windows; a solitary blind like this, covering just one pane, is usually a sign that someone is sitting behind it. One forenoon I stood at the window in the confectioner's over on the other side. It was just twelve o'clock. Without paying attention to the passersby, I stood looking fixedly at this blind, when suddenly the dark shadow behind it began to move. A female head appeared in profile at the next pane, so that it turned, strangely, in the direction in which the blind was facing. Thereupon the owner of the head nodded in a very friendly manner and hid herself again behind the blind. First of all, I inferred that the person she greeted was a man, for her movement was too excited to be evoked by the sight of a girl friend; secondly, I inferred that the person the greeting was meant for usually came from the other direction. For then she had positioned herself quite correctly so as to see him well in advance, indeed to greet him while still concealed by the blind. – Quite right, at twelve precisely comes the hero in this little love scene, our dear lieutenant. I'm sitting in the confectioner's which is on the ground floor of the building whose first floor is occupied by the young lady. The lieutenant has already caught sight of her. Careful now, my friend, it isn't so easy to bow gracefully to a first floor. Well, he's not so bad really; well-grown, erect, a handsome figure, arched nose, dark hair, the tricorn suits him. Now for the dilemma. The knees begin to chatter just a little from standing too long. Its impression on the eye can be compared to the feeling one has when one has toothache and the teeth become too long in the mouth. If you gather all your strength in the eye and direct it at the first floor, you take a little too much energy from the legs. Excuse me, lieutenant, for resting that glance on its Ascension. Yes, I know quite well, it's an impertinence. One can hardly call the glance meaningful, meaningless rather, yet very promising. But these many promises clearly go too much to his head; he totters, to use the poet's words about Agnete, he sways, he falls. That's rough, and if you ask me, it should never have happened. He's too good for that. Really it's fatal, for if you want to impress the ladies as a gallant you must never fall down. If you want to be a gallant you must watch out for things like that. But if you want to appear merely as someone of intelligence, all this is of no consequence; one slumps, one collapses, if one should then actually fall, there is nothing remarkable about that. – What impression can this incident have made on my little lady? It is unfortunate that I cannot be on both sides of the Dardanelles at once. I could of course have an acquaintance posted on the other side, but on the one hand, I always like to make my own observations, and on the other, one can never tell what there might be in this story for me, and in that case it is never good to have a confidant, since one then has to waste time getting out of him what he knows and confusing him. – Really I am beginning to grow tired of my good lieutenant. Day after day he comes by in full uniform. How terribly unflinching! Is that kind of thing fitting for a soldier? My dear sir, don't you carry a sword or a bayonet? Shouldn't you take the house by storm and the girl by force? Yes, if you were a student, a licenciate, a curate living on hope, it would be different. Still, I forgive you, for the girl pleases me the more I look at her. She is pretty, her brown eyes are full of mischief. When she waits for your arrival her appearance glows with a heightened beauty that is indescribably becoming. I infer from this that she must have a great deal of imagination, and imagination is the natural rouge of the fair sex.

My Cordelia!

What is longing [*Længsel*]? Language and the poets rhyme

it with the word 'prison' [*Fængsel*]. How absurd! As though only someone sitting in gaol could long for something. As if one couldn't long for something when one is free! If I were set free, would I not long? But then, of course, I am free, free as a bird, but how much I long! I long when I am on my way to you; I long when I leave you, I long for you even when I sit by your side. Can one long for what one has? Yes, when you consider that the next moment you may not have it. My longing is an eternal impatience. Only after living through all eternity and assuring myself that you were mine every instant, only then would I return to you and live with you through all eternity, and no doubt not have patience enough to be separated from you for an instant without longing, but assurance enough to sit calmly at your side.

Your Johannes

My Cordelia!

Outside the door stands a cabriolet, for me bigger than all the world, since it is large enough for two, hitched to a pair of horses, wild and unmanageable as natural forces, impatient as my passions, bold as your thoughts. If it's your wish, I shall carry you off – my Cordelia! Is it your command? Your command is the password that loosens the reins and sets free flight's desire. I carry you off, not from one lot of people to another, but out of the world – the horses rear, the chaise rises; the horses stand almost vertically over us; we drive heavenwards through the clouds, the wind roars about us; is it we who sit still and the whole world that is moving, or is it our bold flight? Does it make you giddy, dear Cordelia? Then hold on to me; I shall not be giddy. When one thinks only of one thing, one never becomes giddy in a spiritual sense, and I am thinking only of you – nor in a bodily sense, for I look only at you. Hold tight: if the world perished, if our light carriage disappeared beneath us, we would still hold each other in our embrace, floating in the harmony of the spheres.

Your Johannes

It's almost too much. My servant has waited six hours, I myself two, in wind and rain, just to be on the lookout for that dear child, Charlotte Hahn. There is an old aunt of hers she usually visits every Wednesday between two and five. Today she doesn't come, just when I wanted so much to see her. And why? Because she puts me in a quite special mood. I greet her, she curtsies in a way at once indescribably earthly yet heavenly; she almost stands still, it's as though she was about to sink into the earth, yet her look is as of one who could be raised up to heaven. When I look at her, my mind becomes at once solemn yet covetous. Otherwise, the girl does not interest me in the least. All I demand is this greeting, nothing more even if she were willing to give it. Her greeting puts me in a mood which I then lavish on Cordelia. – And yet I'll bet that some way or another she has given us the slip. It is difficult, not just in comedies but in real life too, to keep track of a young girl; one needs an eye in every finger. There was a nymph, Cardea, who meddled in fooling men. She lived in woods, lured her lovers into the thickest brush, and vanished. She wanted to fool Janus too, but he fooled her, for he had eyes in the back of his head.

*

My letters do not fail of their purpose. They are developing her mentally, if not erotically. For that I have to use notes. The more prominent the erotic becomes, the shorter the notes will be, but all the more certain to grasp the erotic point. Nevertheless, in order not to make her sentimental or soft, irony stiffens her feelings again, but also gives her an appetite for the nourishment most dear to her. The notes give distant and vague hints of the highest. The moment this presentiment begins to dawn in her soul, the relationship fractures. Through my resistance, the presentiment takes shape in her soul as though it were her own thought, her own heart's inclination. It's just what I want.

My Cordelia!
    Somewhere in town there lives a little family consisting of a widow and three daughters. Two of these go to the Royal

Kitchens to learn to cook. It is spring, about five one afternoon, the drawing-room door opens softly, a reconnoitring glance looks about the room. There is no one, just a young girl sitting at the piano. The door is ajar so one can listen unnoticed. It is no artist playing, for then the door would have been shut. She is playing a Swedish melody, about the ephemeral quality of youth and beauty. The words mock the girl's own youth and beauty; the girl's youth and beauty mock the words. Which of them is right, the girl or the words? The tones are so quiet, so melancholy, as though sadness were the arbitrator who would settle the dispute. – But it is wrong, this sadness! What association is there between youth and reflections of this kind, what fellowship between morning and evening? The keys vibrate and tremble, the spirits of the sounding-board rise in confusion and do not understand one another – my Cordelia, why so vehement! To what end this passion?

How far removed in time must an event be for us to remember it? How far for memory's longing to be no longer able to seize it? Most people have a limit in this respect: what lies too near them in time they cannot remember, nor what lies too remote. I know no limit. What was experienced yesterday, I push back a thousand years in time, and remember it as if it were yesterday.

Your Johannes

My Cordelia!

I have a secret to confide to you, my confidante. Who should I confide it to? To Echo? She would betray it. To the stars? They are cold. People? They do not understand. Only to you can I confide it, for you know how to safeguard it. There is a girl, more beautiful than my soul's dream, purer than the light of the sun, deeper than the source of the ocean, more proud than the flight of the eagle – there is a girl – oh! bend your head to my ear and my words, that my secret may steal into it – this girl I love more dearly than my life, for she is my life; more dearly than all my desires, for she is the only one; more dearly than all my thoughts, for she is the only one; more warmly than the sun loves the flower, more intensely than sorrow the privacy of the troubled mind; more longingly than the desert's burning sand loves the rain – I cling to her more tenderly than the mother's eye to the child, more confidingly than the pleading soul to God, more inseparably than the plant to its root. – Your head grows heavy and thoughtful, it sinks down on your breast, your bosom rises to its aid – my Cordelia! You have understood me, you have understood me exactly, to the letter, not one jot have you ignored! Shall I stretch the membrane of my ear and let your voice assure me of this? Should I doubt? Will you safeguard this secret? Can I depend on you? One hears of people who, in terrible crimes, dedicate themselves to mutual silence. I have confided to you a secret which is my life and my life's content. Have you nothing to confide to me, nothing so beautiful, so significant, so chaste, that supernatural forces would be set in motion if it were betrayed?

Your Johannes

My Cordelia!

The sky is overcast – it is furrowed with dark rain-clouds, like dark brows above its passionate countenance; the trees in the forest stir, unsettled by troubled dreams. You have vanished from me in the forest. Behind every tree I see a womanly being that resembles you; when I get nearer, it hides behind the next tree. Won't you reveal yourself to me, not gather yourself together? Everything is in confusion before me; the single parts of the forest lose their separate outlines, I see everything as a sea of fog, where womanly beings resembling you everywhere appear and disappear. But you I do not see, you are always moving on the waves of intuition, and yet even every single resemblance of you makes me happy. What is the reason? – Is it the rich unity of your being or the impoverished multiplicity of mine? – Is not loving you to love a world?

Your Johannes

It would really be interesting, if it were possible, to keep an exact record of my conversations with Cordelia. But I see very clearly that it is not possible. For even if I managed to remember every word exchanged between us, it would still be impossible to convey the contemporaneity that is really the nerve of our conversation, the element of surprise in the outburst, the animation that is conversation's life-principle. Nor, as a rule, of course, have I prepared myself, which would also go against the real nature of conversation, particularly erotic conversation. All that I have constantly in mind is the content of my letters, and constantly in view the mood these might possibly evoke in her. Naturally, it could never occur to me to ask her if she had read my letter. I can easily prove to myself that she has read it. Nor do I ever talk to her of this directly, but keep up a secretive communication with the letters in my conversations, partly to implant some impression or other more deeply in her soul, partly to take it away from her again and leave her undecided. Then she can read the letter again and get a new impression from it, and so on.

A change has taken place in her, and is taking place. Were I to describe the state of her soul at this moment, I would call it pantheistic daring. Her glance betrays it straightaway. It is bold, almost foolhardy in its expectation, as if every instant it demanded and was prepared to behold the supernatural. Like an eye that sees beyond itself, this glance travels beyond what appears immediately before it and beholds the marvellous. It is bold, almost foolhardy in its expectation but not in its self-confidence; it is therefore something dreaming and imploring, not proud and commanding. She seeks the marvellous outside herself, she prays for it to appear, as if it was not in her own power to evoke it. This must be prevented, otherwise I shall gain the ascendancy over her too soon. She said to me yesterday that there was something regal in my nature. Perhaps she wants to submit; that won't do at all. Certainly, my dear Cordelia, there is something regal in my nature, but you have no idea what kind of kingdom it is I rule over. It is over the storms of moods. Like Aeolus, I keep them shut up in my personal mountain and let now one, now another, go forth. Flattery will give her self-esteem; the difference between mine and thine will become effective; everything is placed on her side. To flatter requires great caution. At times one must set oneself up very high but in a way that leaves room for a place still higher; at times one must set oneself down very low. The former is the more correct in moving in the direction of the spiritual, the latter in moving towards the erotic. – Does she owe me anything? Nothing at all. Could I wish that she did? Not at all. I am too much a connoisseur, and know the erotic too well, for any such tomfoolery. If that were actually the case, I should endeavour with all my might to make her forget it, and hush my own thoughts about it to sleep. In relation to the labyrinth of her heart, every young girl is an Ariadne; she owns the thread by which one can find one's way through it, but she owns it without herself knowing how to use it.

My Cordelia!

Speak – I obey. Your wish is my command. Your prayer is an all-powerful invocation, your every fleeting wish my benefaction; for I obey you not as an obliging spirit, as though I stood outside you. When you command, your will takes shape, and with it myself, for I am a confusion of soul that simply awaits your word.

Your Johannes

My Cordelia!

You know I am very fond of talking to myself. In myself I have found the most interesting of my acquaintances. I have sometimes feared that I might come to lack topics for these conversations of mine; now I have no fear, now I have you. I talk, then, to myself, now and to all eternity about you, about the most interesting subject to the most interesting person – alas! for I am only an interesting person, you the most interesting subject.

Your Johannes

My Cordelia!

You think it is such a short time I have loved you; you seem almost afraid that I may have loved someone before. There is a certain kind of handwriting in which the well-favoured eye immediately suspects an older hand, which in the course of time has been supplanted by empty foolishness. With corrosive chemicals this later writing is erased and the original then stands out plain and clear. Similarly, your eye has taught me, within myself, to find myself; I let oblivion consume all that has nothing to do with you, and then I discover an ancient, a divinely young, elemental hand; I discover that my love for you is as old as myself.

Your Johannes

My Cordelia!

How can a kingdom stand which is divided against itself? How am I going to be able to keep going when I am in two minds? What about? About you, to find rest if possible in the thought that I am in love with you. But how to find this rest? One of the contesting powers wants constantly to persuade the other that it is the one most deeply and heartily in love; the next moment the other does the same. I wouldn't be greatly troubled if I had the struggle outside me, if there was someone else who dared to be in love with you, or dared not to be, the crime is equally great; but this struggle within my own being consumes me, this one passion in its ambivalence.

Your Johannes

*

Just be off with you, my little fisher-girl; just hide yourself among the trees; just take up your burden, bending down suits you well; yes, even at this moment it is with a natural grace you bend down under the firewood you have collected – that such a creature should bear such burdens! Like a dancer you reveal your beautiful contours – slender waist, broad bosom, burgeoning, any enrolment officer must admit that. Maybe you think it's all unimportant, you think that the fine ladies are far more beautiful. Ah, my child! You do not know how much deception there is in the world. Just begin your journey with your burden into the huge forest, which presumably stretches many, many miles into the country, right up to the blue mountains. Maybe you are not a real fisher-girl but an enchanted princess; you are the servant of a troll; he is cruel enough to make you fetch firewood in the forest. That's how it always is in fairy stories. Why else do you go deeper into the forest? If you are a real fisher-girl, you should go down to the bothy with your firewood, past me as I stand on the other side of the road. – Just follow the footpath which winds playfully through the trees, my eyes will find you; just turn and look at me, my eyes are following you; you cannot move me, no longing carries me away, I sit calmly on the fence and smoke my cigar. – Some other time – perhaps. – Yes, your glance is roguish when you half turn your head back that way; your graceful walk inviting – yes, I know, I realize where this path leads – to the solitude of the forest, to the murmur of the trees, to the manifold stillness. Look, heaven itself befriends you, it hides in the clouds, it darkens the background of the forest, it is as if it drew the curtain for us. – Farewell, my pretty fisher-girl, live well. Thanks for your favour, it was a beautiful moment, a mood not strong enough to move me from my firm place on the railing, yet rich in inward emotion.

*

When Jacob had bargained with Laban about the payment for his services, when they had agreed that Jacob should watch the white sheep, and as return for his work should have the speckled lambs which were born in his flock, he laid sticks in the water troughs and let the sheep gaze at them. Similarly, I place myself everywhere before Cordelia, her eye sees me constantly. To her it seems nothing but attentiveness on my part: for my part, however, I know that her soul is losing interest in everything else, that there is developing within her a spiritual concupiscence which sees me everywhere.

My Cordelia!

If I could forget you! Is my love then a work of memory? Even if time expunged everything from its tablets, expunged even memory itself, my relation to you would stay just as alive, you would still not be forgotten. If I could forget you! What then should I remember? For after all, I have forgotten myself in order to remember you; so if I forgot you I would come to remember myself; but the moment I remembered myself I would have to remember you again. If I could forget you! What would happen then? There is a picture from antiquity. It depicts Ariadne. She is leaping up from her couch and gazing anxiously after a ship that is hurrying away under full sail. By her side stands Cupid with unstrung bow and drying his eyes. Behind her stands a winged female figure in a helmet. It is usually assumed this is Nemesis. Imagine this picture, imagine it changed a little. Cupid is not weeping and his bow is not unstrung; or would you have become less beautiful, less victorious, if I had become mad? Cupid smiles and bends his bow. Nemesis does not stand inactive by your side; she too draws her bow. In that other picture we see a male figure on the ship, busily occupied. It is assumed it is Theseus. Not so in my picture. He stands on the stern, he looks back longingly, spreads his arms. He has repented, or rather, his madness has left him, but the ship carries him away. Cupid and Nemesis both aim at him, an arrow flies from each bow; their aim is true; one sees that, one understands, they have both hit the same place in his heart, as a sign that his love was the Nemesis that wrought vengeance.

Your Johannes

My Cordelia!

In love with myself, that is what people say I am. It doesn't surprise me, for how could they notice that I can love when I love only you; how could anyone else suspect it when I love only you? In love with myself. Why? Because I'm in love with you, because it is you I love, you alone, and all that truly belongs to you, and it is thus I love myself, because this, my self, belongs to you, so that if I ceased loving you I would cease loving myself. What then is, in the eyes of the profane world, an expression of the greatest egoism, is for your initiated eyes the expression of purest sympathy; what in the profane eyes of the world is an expression of the most prosaic self-preservation, is for your sacred sight the expression of the most enthusiastic self-annihilation.

Your Johannes

What I feared most was that the whole process might take me too long. I see, however, that Cordelia is making great progress; yes, that it will be necessary to mobilize everything to keep her mind on the job. She mustn't for all the world lose interest before time, that is, before the time when time has passed for her.

*

If one loves, one does not follow the main road. It is only marriage that keeps to the middle of the king's highway. If one loves and takes a walk from Nøddebo, one doesn't go along Esrom Lake even though really it's just a hunting track; but it is a beaten track and love prefers to beat its own. One penetrates deeper into Grib's Forest. And when one wanders thus, arm in arm, one understands each other; what before vaguely delighted and pained becomes clear. One has no idea anyone is present. – So that lovely beech tree became a witness to your love; you first confessed it beneath its crown. You remembered everything so clearly. That first time you saw each other, when you held out your hands to each other in the dance, the first time you parted near dawn, when you would admit nothing to yourselves, least of all to each other. – It's really rather beautiful listening to these rehearsals of love. – They fell on their knees under the tree, they swore inviolable love to each other, they sealed the pact with the first kiss. – These are fruitful moods that must be lavished on Cordelia. – So this beech was a witness. Oh yes! a tree is a very suitable witness, but still not enough. You think, perhaps, the sky was also a witness, yet the sky in itself is a very abstract idea. But as far as that goes, there is still a witness. Ought I to stand up, let them see I am here? No, they might know me and that would ruin things. Should I stand up when they leave, let them realize there was someone there? No, there's no point in that. Let silence rest over their secret – as long as I please. They're in my power, I can separate them when I want. I am in on their secret; it is only from her or from him that I could have learnt it – from her, that's impossible – so from him – that's abhorrent – bravo! yet it's really almost spite. Well, I'll see. If I can get a definite impression of her in the normal way, as I prefer, but usually I can't, then there's nothing else for it.

My Cordelia!

I am poor – you are my riches; dark – you are my light; I own nothing, need nothing. And how could I own anything? After all, it is a contradiction that he can own something who does not own himself. I am happy as a child who is neither able to own anything nor allowed to. I own nothing, for I belong only to you; I am not, I have ceased to be, in order to be yours.

Your Johannes

My Cordelia!

'Mine': what does this word mean? Not what belongs to me, but what I belong to, what contains my whole being, which is mine only so far as I belong to it. My God is not the God that belongs to me, but the God to whom I belong; and so, too, when I say my native land, my home, my calling, my longing, my hope. If there had been no immortality before, this thought that I am yours would be a breach of the normal course of nature.

Your Johannes

My Cordelia!

What am I? The modest narrator who accompanies your

triumphs; the dancer who supports you when you rise in your lovely grace; the branch upon which you rest a moment when you are tired of flying; the bass that interposes itself below the soprano's fervour to let it climb even higher – what am I? I am the earthly gravity that keeps you on the ground. What am I, then? Body, mass, earth, dust and ashes. – You, my Cordelia, you are soul and spirit.

Your Johannes

My Cordelia!

Love is everything. So, for one who loves, everything has ceased to have meaning in itself and only means something through the interpretation love gives it. Thus if another betrothed became convinced there was some other girl he cared for, he would presumably stand there like a criminal and his fiancée be outraged. You, however, I know would see a tribute in such a confession; for me to be able to love another you know is an impossibility; it is my love for you casting its reflection over the whole of life. So when I care about someone else, it is not to convince myself that I do not love her but only you – that would be presumptuous; but since my whole soul is filled with you, life takes on another meaning for me: it becomes a myth about you.

Your Johannes

My Cordelia!

My love consumes me. Only my voice is left, a voice which has fallen in love with you whispers to you everywhere that I love you. Oh! does it weary you to hear this voice? Everywhere it enfolds you; like an inexhaustible, shifting surround, I place my transparently reflected soul about your pure, deep being.

Your Johannes

My Cordelia!

One reads in ancient tales how a river fell in love with a girl. Similarly, my soul is a river which loves you. At one

99

moment it is peaceful and allows your image to be reflected in it deeply and undistorted; at another it fancies it has captured your image, and its waves foam to prevent you getting away; sometimes it softly ruffles its surface and plays with your reflection, sometimes it loses it, and then its waves become dark and despairing. – That's how my soul is: like a river that has fallen in love with you.

Your Johannes

*

Frankly, without an exceptionally vivid imagination one could conceive of a more convenient, comfortable, and above all more elegant means of transport; riding with a peat-carrier creates a stir only in metaphorical sense. – But at a pinch one accepts it with thanks. One goes some way down the highway, one sets oneself up on the cart, one rides five miles or so and meets nothing, ten miles and everything's going fine: one becomes calm and secure; really the scenery looks better than usual from this position. One has come almost fifteen miles – now who would have expected, so far out here on the highway, to meet someone from Copenhagen? And it is someone from Copenhagen, you can see that all right, it's no countryman; he looks at you in a quite special way, so assured, so observant, so appraising, and a little scornful. Yes, my dear girl, your position is by no means comfortable; you look as if you were sitting on a serving-tray, the wagon is so flat that it has no hollow for your feet. But it's your own fault; my carriage is entirely at your service. I venture to offer you a much less embarrassing place, unless it would embarrass you to sit by my side. If so, I would leave the whole carriage to you and sit in the driver's seat myself, pleased to be allowed to convey you to your destination. – The straw hat isn't quite adequate protection against a sideways glance. It's no good your bending down your head, I can still admire the lovely profile. – Isn't it annoying, the peasant greeting me? But after all it's quite proper for a peasant to show respect to a distinguished man. – You can't get out of it like that; here's a tavern, yes, a staging-post, and a peat-carrier is in his own way too pious not to attend to his devotions. I'll take care of him. I have an exceptional talent for charming peat-carriers. May I be so fortunate as to please you too! He won't be able to resist my offer, and when he has accepted it he won't be able to resist its effect. If I can't do it, my servant can. There, he's going into the tap-room now; you are alone on the wagon in the shelter. – Heaven only knows what kind of young girl this is. Could she be a little middle-class girl, perhaps a deacon's daughter? If so, for a deacon's daughter she is uncommonly pretty, and dressed with unusual taste. The deacon must have a good living. It occurs to me, might she not be a little thoroughbred who has tired of riding in her equipage, who has perhaps gone for a little hike out to the country house, and now wants to try her hand at a little adventure too? Certainly possible, such things are not unheard of. – The peasant doesn't know a thing; he is a numbskull who knows only how to drink: yes, yes, just drink, old chap, he's welcome to it. – But what do I see in there? Miss Jespersen, no less, Hansine Jespersen, daughter of the wholesaler. God preserve us! We two know each other. It was her I once met on Bredgade, she was sitting on a seat facing backwards and she couldn't get the window up; I put on my glasses and then had the pleasure of following her with my eyes. It was a very confined position, there were so many in the carriage that she couldn't move, and she presumably didn't dare to cause a scene. The present position is just as awkward, to be sure. Clearly we two are predestined for each other. She's supposed to be a romantic little girl; she is definitely out on her own. – There comes my servant with the peat-carrier. He is completely drunk. It's disgusting; they're a depraved lot, these peat-carriers. Yes, alas! Yet there are worse people than peat-carriers. See, now you are going to have to drive anyway. You will have to drive the horses yourself; it is quite romantic. You refuse my invitation. You insist you are a very good driver. You do not deceive me. I can see well enough how sly you are. When you have gone a little way, you will jump off, it's easy to find a hiding-place in the forest. – My horse must be saddled, I shall follow you on horseback. – There, look! now I am ready, now you can feel safe against any assault. – But don't be so frightfully afraid, or I'll turn back immediately. I only want to frighten you a little and provide an opportunity for your natural beauty to be heightened. You don't know, indeed, that it was I who let the peasant get drunk, and I have not permitted myself a single offensive remark. Everything can still be fine; I shall no doubt give the affair a twist which will let you laugh at the whole story. All I want is a little settling of accounts with you. Never believe I would take any young girl off her guard. I am a friend of freedom, and whatever does not come to me freely I do not bother with at all. – 'You will certainly realize that you cannot continue your journey in this manner. I myself am going hunting, that's why I'm on horseback. However, my carriage is ready at the tavern. If you so command, it will catch up with you in an instant and take you where you want. I am myself unfortunately unable to have the pleasure of accompanying you, for I am bound by a hunting promise, and they are sacred.' – But you accept – everything will be arranged in an instant. – Now you see you needn't at all be embarrassed at seeing me again, or at least not more embarrassed than well suits you. You can amuse yourself with the whole story, laugh a little and think a little about me. More I do not ask. It may not seem very much; for me it is enough. It is the beginning, and I am especially strong on rudiments.

*

Yesterday evening the aunt had a small party. I knew Cordelia would take out her knitting. I had hidden a little note in it. She lost it, picked it up, became excited and wistful. This is how one should always exploit the situation. It is incredible the advantages you can derive from it. A note of no consequence in itself, read in these circumstances, becomes for her infinitely important. She got no chance to talk with me; I had arranged it so that I had to escort a lady home. So Cordelia had to wait until today. That's always a good way of letting an impression bury itself all the deeper in her soul. It looks all the time as if it were I that was showing her attention. The advantage I have is that I am given a place in her thoughts everywhere, surprise her everywhere.

Love, however, has its own dialectic. There was a young girl

I was once in love with. Last summer at the theatre in Dresden I saw an actress who bore a deceptive resemblance to her. Because of this I wanted to make her acquaintance, and succeeded, and then convinced myself that there was a quite considerable difference all the same. Today I met a lady on the street who reminded me of that actress. This story can go on as long as you like.

Everywhere my thoughts encircle Cordelia, I place them around her like guardian angels. As Venus is drawn in her chariot by doves, she sits in her triumphal car and I harness my thoughts to it like winged creatures. She herself sits there happy, rich as a child, omnipotent as a goddess; I walk by her side. Truly, a young girl is after all, and remains, a *venerabile* of Nature and of all existence! That's something no one knows better than I. The only pity is that this glory is so short-lived. She smiles at me, she greets me, she beckons to me as if she were my sister. A single glance reminds her that she is my beloved.

Love has many positionings. Cordelia makes good progress. She is sitting on my lap, her arm twines, soft and warm, round my neck; she leans upon my breast, light, without gravity; the soft contours scarcely touch me; like a flower her lovely figure twines about me, freely as a ribbon. Her eyes are hidden beneath her lashes, her bosom is dazzling white like snow, so smooth that my eye cannot rest, it would glance off if her bosom were not moving. What does this movement mean? Is it love? Perhaps. It is a presentiment of it, its dream. It still lacks energy. Her embrace is comprehensive, as the cloud enfolding the transfigured one, detached as a breeze, soft as the fondling of a flower; she kisses me unspecifically, as the sky kisses the sea, gently and quietly, as the dew kisses a flower, solemnly as the sea kisses the image of the moon.

I would call her passion at this moment a naive passion. When the change has been made and I begin to draw back in earnest, she will call on everything she has to captivate me. She has no other means for this purpose than the erotic itself, except that this will now appear on a quite different scale. It then becomes a weapon in her hand which she wields against me. I then have the reflected passion. She fights for her own sake because she knows I possess the erotic; she fights for her own sake so as to overcome me. She herself is in need of a higher form of the erotic. What I taught her to suspect by arousing her, my coldness now teaches her to understand but in such a way that she thinks it is she herself who discovers it. So she wants to take me by surprise; she wants to believe that she has outstripped me in audacity, and that makes me her prisoner. Her passion then becomes specific, energetic, conclusive, dialectical; her kiss total, her embrace without hesitation. – In me she seeks her freedom and finds it the better the more firmly I encompass her. The engagement bursts. When that has happened she needs a little rest, so that nothing unseemly will emerge from this wild tumult. Her passion then composes itself once more and she is mine.

Just as I had already supervised her reading indirectly in the time of Edvard of blessed memory, so now I do that directly. What I offer her is what I consider the best nourishment: mythology and fairy-tales. She is nevertheless free in this as in everything; there is nothing that I have not learned from her herself. If it isn't there to begin with, I first put it there.

*

When the servant girls go to the Zoological Gardens in the summer, generally the Gardens offer but poor entertainment. The girls go there only once a year and so feel they must really make the most of it. They have to put on hat and shawl and disfigure themselves in every way. Their gaiety is wild, unseemly and lascivious. No, I count then on Frederiksberg Gardens. It's on Sunday afternoons they come there, and I too. Here everything is seemly and decent, the gaiety itself quieter and more refined. In general, the man who doesn't appreciate servant girls has more to lose than they. The servant girls' motley host is really the most beautiful civil guard we have in Denmark. If I were king, I know what I would do – I wouldn't review the regulars. If I were a city alderman I should immediately move to have a welfare committee appointed to strive to encourage the servant girls in every possible way, by insight, advice, exhortation and suitable rewards, to get themselves up with taste and care. Why should beauty go to waste? Why should it go through life unnoticed? At least let it appear once a week in the light that shows it to best advantage! But above all, taste, restraint. A servant girl should not look like a lady, so far I agree with *Politivennen*, but the reasons that respectable paper adduces are altogether mistaken. If we could anticipate a desirable flourishing of the servant class in this way, wouldn't this in turn have a beneficial effect on our houses' daughters? Or is it too bold of me to espy a future for Denmark which can truly be called matchless? If only I myself were lucky enough to be that golden age's contemporary, the whole day could be spent with a good conscience in the streets and alleys rejoicing in the pleasures of the eye. What broad and bold, what patriotic daydreams! But here I am in Frederiksberg Gardens where the servant girls come on Sunday afternoon, and I too. – First come the country girls, hand in hand with their sweethearts; or in another formation, girls all in front hand in hand, men all behind; or in another, two girls and one man. This throng forms the frame; they usually stand or sit along by the trees in the big quadrangle in front of the pavilion. They are hale and hearty, just the colour clashes are a little too strong, in their dress as well as their complexions. Inside this frame now come the servant girls from Jutland and Fyn: tall, straight, a little too stalwart, their dress a little confused. Here there would be much for the committee to do. Nor does one want for the occasional representative of the Bornholm division: capable cooks, but not very approachable either in the kitchen or in Frederiksberg; there is something proudly forbidding about them. The contrast their presence offers is therefore not without its effect, and I'd rather not be without them out here, though I rarely have anything to do with them. – Now follow the core troops, the girls from Nyboder. Smaller in stature, plump, with a full figure, delicate complexion, gay, happy, sprightly, talkative, a little coquettish and above all, bareheaded. Their dress can well approximate to a lady's; just two things to notice, they don't have a shawl but a kerchief, no hat but a little smart cap at most, they should preferably be bareheaded. – Why, hello, Marie! Fancy meeting you here! It's been a long time. Are you still at the Counsellor's? – 'Yes' – An excellent situation, isn't it? – 'Yes' – But you are so alone out here, no one to accompany . . . no sweetheart, perhaps he hasn't had time today, or you're waiting for him? – What, you aren't engaged? Impossible. The prettiest girl in Copenhagen, a girl in service at the Counsellor's, a girl who is an embellishment and an example to all servant girls, a girl who knows how to dress so prettily and . . . so opulently. What an exquisite little handkerchief you have in your hand, of the finest cambric . . . and what do I see, embroidery on the edges? I bet it cost ten marks . . . you can be sure there's many a fine lady who doesn't own its equal . . . French gloves . . . a silk parasol . . . and a girl like that not engaged? . . . It's absurd. Unless my memory is letting me down badly, Jens was pretty fond of you. You must know Jens, the wholesaler's Jens, on the second floor . . . See, I got it right . . . So why didn't you get engaged? Jens was a handsome fellow, he had a good situation, with the Counsellor's influence he might have made a policeman or fireman in due course; it wouldn't have been such a bad match . . . The fault must definitely be yours, you've been too hard on him . . . 'No!, but I found out Jens had been engaged once before to a girl they say he didn't treat nicely at all.' – . . . No, you don't say; who would have believed Jens was such a naughty rascal . . . yes, these Guards fellows . . . these Guards fellows aren't to be depended on . . . You did quite right, a girl like you is altogether too good to be thrown away on just anybody . . . You can be sure you'll make a better match, I'll guarantee it. – How is Miss Juliane? I haven't seen her for some time. I'm sure my pretty Marie could help me with a little information . . . just because one has been unhappy in love oneself one needn't lack sympathy for others . . . There are so many people here . . . I daren't talk to you about it, I'm afraid in case someone spies on me . . . Listen just a moment, my pretty Marie . . . Look, here's the place, in this shaded walk, where the trees twine round each other so as to hide us from others, where we see no one else, hear no human voice but only a soft echo of the music . . . here I dare to speak of my secret . . . Now, if Jens hadn't been a bad man, you'd have walked with him here arm in arm, wouldn't you, and listened to the joyful music, and enjoyed an even greater happiness yourself . . . why so moved? – Just forget Jens . . . Don't get me wrong . . . it was to meet you I came out here . . . It was to see you that I came to the Counsellor's . . . You surely noticed . . . Whenever I could I always passed the kitchen door . . . You must be mine . . . The banns shall be published . . . tomorrow evening I will explain everything . . . up the backstairs, the door to the left, right across from the kitchen . . . Goodbye, my pretty Marie . . . don't let anyone know you have seen me out here or spoken with me. You know my secret. – She is really delightful, something might be made of her. – If I ever get a foothold in her chamber I'll announce those banns myself. I have always tried to develop that beautiful Greek autarchy and in particular make the priest superfluous.

*

If I could stand behind Cordelia when she received a letter from me, it might be very interesting. Then I could convince myself more easily how far she had taken them in erotically in the most literal sense. On the whole, letters are and will always be an invaluable means for making an impression upon a young girl; often the dead symbol has far greater influence than the living word. A letter is a secret communication; you are master of the situation, feel no pressure from anyone's presence, and I think a young girl would really rather be quite alone with her ideal, that is, at particular moments, and precisely when it is influencing her mind most strongly. Even if her ideal has found a fairly complete expression in a definite object of love, there are still moments when she feels that there is an excess in the ideal that reality lacks. These great feasts of the atonement must be granted to her; only one must be careful to use them in the right way, so that she does not return to reality from them weakened but strengthened. Here a letter helps; its effect is that one is invisibly but spiritually present at these sacred moments of consecration, while the idea that the real person is the author of the letter creates a natural and easy transition to reality.

Could I become jealous of Cordelia? Damn it, yes! Though in another sense, no! For if I saw that even if I won my fight against the other, her nature would be disturbed and not what I wanted – then I would give her up.

An old philosopher has said that if you accurately record all that you experience, before you know it you are a philosopher. For some time now I have lived in association with the community of the betrothed. Such a relationship ought then to bear at least some fruit. So I have considered gathering material for a book, entitled *Contribution to the Theory of the Kiss*, dedicated to all tender lovers. It is remarkable, besides, that no work on this subject exists. So if I manage to complete it I will also be fulfilling a long-felt need. Could the reason for this gap in the literature be that philosophers do not consider such matters, or is it that they do not understand them? – I can offer several suggestions right away. The perfect kiss requires that the agents involved be a man and a girl. A kiss between men is in poor taste, or what is worse, distasteful. – Secondly, I believe a kiss comes closer to its concept when a man kisses a girl than when a girl kisses a man. Where in the course of years the distinction in this relation is lost sight of, the kiss loses its significance. This is true of the domestic kiss with which married people, for want of napkins, wipe each other on the mouth while saying, 'You're welcome.' – If the age difference is very large, the kiss falls outside the concept. I remember in a girls' school, in one of the provinces, the oldest class had its own saying: 'to kiss the counsellor', an expression with which they associated an idea that was anything but agreeable. It began like this: the schoolmistress had a brother-in-law living in her house. He had been a counsellor, was an elderly man, and took advantage of his age to kiss the young girls. – The kiss must be an expression of a definite passion. When a brother and sister who are twins kiss each other, that is not a proper kiss. The same is true of kisses that are bonuses from Christmas games, likewise a stolen kiss. A kiss is a symbolic action which lacks meaning when the feeling it should indicate is not present, and this feeling can only be present under certain conditions. – If one wants to try classifying the kiss, one can conceive of several principles of classification. They can be classified according to sound. Unfortunately, here language is not adequate to my observations. I don't believe all the languages in the world have an adequate supply of onomatopoeias to cover the distinctions I have come to recognize just in my uncle's house. Sometimes it is clicking, sometimes hissing, sometimes smacking, sometimes popping, sometimes rumbling, sometimes resonant, sometimes hollow, sometimes like calico, and so on. One can classify the kiss according to the form of contact, as in the tangential kiss, or kiss *en passant*, and the clinging kiss. One can classify them with reference to time, the brief and the prolonged. There is also, with reference to time, another classification, and it is the only one I have really cared about. Thus a distinction is made between the first kiss and all others. What reflection focuses on here is incommensurable with what the other classifications bring to light; it is indifferent to sound, touch, time in general. But the first kiss is qualitatively different from all others. Few people consider this; a pity if there were not one who thinks about it.

My Cordelia!

A good answer is like a sweet kiss, says Solomon. You know I am given to asking questions. People almost take me to task for it. That's because they do not understand what I ask; for you and you alone understand what it is I ask, and you and you alone understand how to answer, and you and you alone understand how to give a good answer; for a good answer is like a sweet kiss, says Solomon.

Your Johannes

There is a difference between a spiritual and a physical eroticism. Up to now it is mostly the spiritual kind I have tried to develop in Cordelia. My physical presence must now be something different, not just the accompanying mood, it must be tempting. I have been constantly preparing myself these days by reading the celebrated passage in the *Phaedrus* on love. It electrifies my whole being and is an excellent prelude. After all, Plato really understood love.

My Cordelia!

Latin says of an attentive disciple that he hangs on his master's lips. For love everything is imagery, and the image in turn is reality. Am I not a diligent, an attentive disciple? But then you aren't saying a word!

Your Johannes

If someone other than I were guiding this process, he would presumably have more sense than to let himself be guided. Were I to consult an initiate among the betrothed, he would probably declare with an access of erotic daring, 'I search in vain in these positionings of love for the sound-image in which the lovers tell of their love.' I would reply, 'I'm glad you seek it in vain, for that image just does not come within the scope of the genuinely erotic, not even if you include the interesting.' Love is far too substantial to make do with chat; erotic situations have far too much meaning in themselves to be supplemented by chat. They are silent, still, in definite contours, and yet eloquent as the music of Memnon's statue. Eros gesticulates, he does not speak; or if he does, it is an enigmatic hint, a symbolic music. Erotic situations are always either sculptural or picturesque; but two people talking together about their love are neither sculptural nor picturesque. The solidly engaged, however, always begin with such small talk, which later also becomes the connecting thread in their garrulous marriage. This small talk is also the beginning and promise of the fact that their marriage will not lack the dowry Ovid speaks of: *dos est uxoria lites.* – If there is talking to be done, it is enough that one of them should do it. The man should do the talking and should therefore possess some of the powers that lay in the girdle of Venus, with which she beguiled men: conversation and sweet flattery, that is to say, the insinuative. It by no means follows that Eros is silent, or that it would be erotically incorrect to converse, only that the conversation itself should be erotic, not lost in edifying observations about prospects in life, and so on, and that it be essentially regarded as a respite from the erotic act, a pastime, not as what is most important. Such a conversation, such a *confabulatio*, is in its nature quite divine, and I never weary of talking with a young girl. That is to say, I can get tired of a particular young girl, but never of talking with a young girl. For me, that is just as impossible as getting tired of breathing. What is the real peculiarity of such a conversation is its vegetative flowering. The conversation stays down to earth, it has no essential topic, the accidental is the law of its movement – but 'a thousand joys' is the name of itself and its produce.

My Cordelia!

'My', 'Your' – these words enclose the humble content of my letters like a parenthesis. Have you noticed that the distance between its arms is getting shorter? Oh, my Cordelia! It is beautiful that the emptier the parenthesis becomes, the fuller it is with meaning.

Your Johannes

My Cordelia!

Is an embrace to be at loggerheads?

Your Johannes

Generally Cordelia keeps silent. This has always pleased me. Her womanly nature is too deep to plague one with hiatus, a figure of speech especially characteristic of the woman and which is unavoidable if the man who is to provide the missing consonants before or after is equally feminine. Occasionally a single brief utterance, however, betrays how much there is in her, and then I can lend a hand. It's as though, behind a person making disconnected stabs at a drawing with an unsure hand, there stood someone else who kept on making out of it something bold and rounded off. She is surprised herself, and yet it seems to be her own. I watch over her, therefore, over every accidental remark, every casually dropped word, and when I give it back to her it has always something more significant in it that she both knows and does not know.

Today we were at a party. We hadn't exchanged a word. We were leaving the table when a servant came in and informed Cordelia that a messenger wished to speak to her. The messenger was from me and brought a letter which contained allusions to a remark I had made at the table. I had managed to introduce it into the general table conversation so that Cordelia, although she sat at a distance from me, couldn't avoid overhearing and misunderstanding it. This is where the letter came in. If I hadn't succeeded in steering the conversation in that direction, I'd have been there in person at the appointed time to confiscate the letter. She came back into the room; she had to tell a little lie. Things like that consolidate the erotic secretiveness without which she cannot make headway down the road onto which she has been directed.

My Cordelia!

Do you believe that he who lays his head on a fairy mound sees the image of the fairy in his dreams? I don't know, but I do know this, that when I rest my head on your breast and don't close my eyes but look out beyond, I see the countenance of an angel. Do you believe that the person who reclines his head on a fairy mound cannot lie still? I don't believe so, but I know that when my head bends to your bosom I am roused too strongly for sleep to fall on my eyes.

Your Johannes

Jacta est alea. The turn must now be made. I was with her today, quite taken with the thought of an idea that entirely occupied me. I had neither eye nor ear for her. The idea itself was interesting and fascinated her too. It would also have been incorrect to begin this new operation by being cold in her presence. Now that I have left and the thought no longer occupies her, she will realize at once that I was different from usual. That it is in her solitude she realizes the change makes this discovery much more painful to her, it acts more slowly but all the more forcibly. She cannot immediately flare up, and when the opportunity arises she has already pondered the thing so much that she cannot find expression for it all in one go but always retains a residue of doubt. The unrest increases, the letters cease, the erotic fare is reduced, the love is scorned as ridiculous. Perhaps she goes along with it for a moment, but in the long run she cannot endure it. She wants now to captivate me with the same means I have used against her, with the erotic.

When it comes to breaking off an engagement every little girl is a great casuist, and although the schools hold no courses on the subject, all young girls are excellently informed of the circumstances in which an engagement should be broken off. It should really be a standard question in the final-year school exams, and while I know there is usually very little variety in essay subjects in girls' schools, I am certain there would be no lack of variation here, since the problem itself offers wide scope for a girl's powers of penetration. And why shouldn't a young girl be given an opportunity to prove her sharpness in the most brilliant manner? Or don't you believe she will get a chance here to show that she is mature enough to – be engaged? I once experienced a situation that interested me very much. At a family's where I sometimes visited, the older members were out one day, but the two young daughters of the house had invited a circle of their girl friends for a morning coffee-party. They were eight in all, all between sixteen and twenty. Presumably they hadn't expected any visitors; the maid had probably been given orders to say no one was at home. I went in all the same and saw clearly they were a little surprised. God knows what eight young girls like that really talk about in a solemn synod of this kind. Married women, too, sometimes gather in similar meetings. Then they discuss pastoral theology, taking up in particular the important questions of when it is most proper to let the maid go to the market alone, whether it is better to have an account with the butcher or pay cash, whether it's likely the cook has a sweetheart and how to put an end to this sweetheart skylarking which causes delays with the cooking. – I found my place in this beautiful cluster. It was very early spring. The sun sent a few scattered rays to herald its arrival. In the room itself everything was wintry, and the scattered rays so annunciative for that very reason. From the table came the aroma of coffee – and then there were the girls themselves, happy, healthy, blooming, and exuberant too, for their anxiety had soon been allayed, and in any case what was there to fear? They were in a way manpower enough. – I managed to draw their attention and the talk to the question of when an engagement should be broken off. While my eye diverted itself by flitting from one flower to the other in this garland of girls, entertaining itself by resting now on one beauty, now on another, my outer ear revelled in the pleasant music of the voices, and the inner ear in listening observantly to what was said. A single word was often enough for me to form a deep insight into the heart of a particular girl, and its history. How seductive, after all, is the road of love! How interesting to find out how far down it the individual has come! I continually fanned the conversation; cleverness, wit, aesthetic objectivity all helped to make the relationship between us more free, yet everything remained within the bounds of strictest decorum. As we thus joked in the free-and-easy atmosphere of conversation, there lay dormant the possibility of a single word of mine causing the good children an unfortunate embarrassment. This possibility was in my power. The girls did not realize it, hardly suspected it. It was suppressed all along by the easy play of conversation, as Scheherazade put off the death sentence by telling stories. Sometimes I led the conversation to the very edge of sadness; sometimes I gave free rein to wantonness; sometimes I tempted them out into a dialectical game. And what material offers more diversity, all depending on how one looks at it? I kept on introducing new themes. – I told of a girl who had been cruelly forced to break off her engagement by her parents. That unhappy collision almost brought tears to their eyes. – I told of someone who had broken off an engagement and given two reasons, that the girl was too large and that he had not gone down on his knees to her when confessing his love. When I had objected to him that these couldn't possibly be considered good enough reasons, he replied, 'Indeed, they are precisely good enough for me to get what I want, for no one can offer a rational answer to that.' I presented a very difficult case for the assembly's consideration. A young girl broke off her engagement because she felt she and her sweetheart were unsuited to each other. The loved one tried to bring her to reason by assuring her how much he loved her, to which she replied: 'Either we are suited to each other and there is real sympathy, and then you will see that we do not suit each other; or we do not suit each other, and then you will see we do not suit each other.' It was amusing to see how the young girls cudgelled their brains to understand this puzzling story, and yet I could see clearly that one or two of them understood it very well, for when it comes to whether to break off an engagement, every young girl is a born casuist. – Yes, I really think I'd find it easier to dispute with the devil himself than with a young girl when it's a question of when one should break off an engagement.

Today I was with her. Quickly, with the speed of thought, I led the conversation to the same subject I had occupied her with yesterday, in a renewed effort to arouse her to an ecstasy. 'There was something I should have mentioned yesterday; it occurred to me after I'd gone.' That succeeded. As long as I am with her she enjoys listening to me; when I've gone she realizes she's been cheated and that I am changed. In this way one extends one's credit. The method is sly but very expedient, like all indirect methods. She has no difficulty in explaining to herself that I myself can be occupied with the sort of things I talk about, and indeed at the time they even interest her, yet I cheat her out of the real erotic.

Oderint, dum metuant. As if only fear and hatred belonged together, while fear and love had nothing at all to do with each other, as if it wasn't fear that made love interesting! What kind of love is it with which we embrace Nature? Isn't there a secret fear and terror in it because Nature's beautiful harmony has to work its way out of lawlessness and wild confusion, its security out of faithlessness? But this anxiety is just what is most fascinating. So too with love if it is to claim our interest. Behind it there should brood the deep, fearful night from which the flower of love springs forth. So rests *nymphaea alba,* with its cup, on the surface of the water, while thought fears to plunge down into the deep darkness where it has its root. – I have noticed, she always calls me *mine* when she writes to me but lacks the courage to say it to me. Today I begged her to do that, as insinuatingly and with as much erotic warmth as I could. She began doing so; an ironic glance, more brief and quicker than you can say it, was enough to make it impossible for her, although my lips urged her with all their might. This mood is normal.

She's mine. I do not confide this to the stars, as is custom and practice. I do not really see what interest those distant spheres can have in this information. Nor do I confide it to any human being, not even to Cordelia. I keep this secret all to myself, whisper it, as it were, to myself, in my most secret conversations with myself. The attempted resistance on her part was not particularly strong; on the other hand the erotic strength she is developing is admirable. How interesting she is in this deep passionateness, how great, almost supernatural! How flexible she is in evasion, how supple in insinuating herself wherever she finds an unfortified point! Everything is mobilized, but in this elemental whirl I find myself precisely in my own element. Yet even in this commotion she is by no means unbeautiful, not torn apart in her moods, not split up into her parts. She is a constant Anadyomene, except that she does not rise up in naive grace or unaffected calm, but stirred by the strong heart-throbs of love, though still in unity and equilibrium. Erotically, she is fully equipped for the struggle; she fights with the shafts of her eyes, with the command of her brow, with the secretiveness of her forehead, with the eloquence of her bosom, with the dangerous attractions of the embrace, with the lips' prayer, with her cheeks' smile, with the sweet longing of her whole form. There is a power in her, an energy, as if she were a Valkyrie; but this erotic vigour is in turn tempered by a certain seductive languor which is exhaled over her. – She must not be held too long at this peak, where only anxiety and unrest can hold her steady and prevent her from falling over. With respect to such emotions she will soon feel that the engagement is too narrow, too confining. She herself will become the tempter who seduces me into going beyond the boundary of the normal; in this way she will become conscious of it herself, and for me that's the main thing.

Not a few remarks are being let fall on her part that suggest she is tired of the engagement. They do not go unheeded; they are my operation's scouts in her soul, which give me informative hints; they're the ends of threads with which I wind her into my plan.

My Cordelia!

You complain about the engagement. You think our love does not need an external bond that only gets in the way. In this I recognize my excellent Cordelia immediately! Truly, I admire you. Our external union is after all nothing but a separation. There is still a partition wall separating us, like Pyramus and Thisbe. That people are privy to it is still a disturbing factor. Only in opposition is there freedom. Only when no outsider suspects it does the love acquire meaning. Only when every stranger believes the lovers hate each other is love happy.

Your Johannes

Soon the bond of betrothal will be broken. She is the one who is unloosening it, to see if by this loosening she can't captivate me still more, as flowing locks are more captivating than those that are bound up. Were I to annul the engagement myself, I would miss this erotic somersault which is so seductive to look at and so sure a sign of her soul's daring. For me that's the main thing. Furthermore, the whole incident would cause me some unpleasantness with others. I would be mistrusted, hated, detested – though unfairly, for think of the advantages it would bring many. Many a little maiden would be quite happy, in the absence of a betrothal, to have come almost that far. That's always something, though, frankly, painfully little because once you have elbowed your way to a place on the expectancy list you have no expectations; the higher one rises on the list, and the further forward one gets, the less prospect there is. In the world of love, the principle of seniority for advancement and promotion does not apply. Furthermore, a little maiden like that is tired of retaining undivided possession; she needs to have her life stirred by an event. But what can compare with an unhappy love affair, especially, too, when she can take the whole thing so lightly? So she lets herself and her neighbour believe she is among the deceived, and since she doesn't qualify for enrolment in a Magdalena Institution, she takes up lodging beside it in a tearful story. One is thus in duty bound to hate me.

Furthermore, there is still another division, of those who have been wholly, or half, or three-quarters, deceived by another. Here there are many degrees, all the way from those who have a ring to show for it to those who can pin their faith on a handshake in a country dance. Their wounds are reopened by the new pain. Their hatred I accept as a bonus. But naturally, to my poor heart all these haters are like so many secret lovers. A king without a country is an absurd figure, but a war of succession between a host of pretenders to a kingdom without a country – that outdoes everything in absurdity. I ought to be loved and cared for by the fair sex as a public pawnbroker. After all, a real fiancé can only take care of one, but such a comprehensive possibility can provide – that is to say, provide more or less – for as many as may be. Then I'm free of all this finite twaddle and also have the advantage of, afterwards, being able to appear in an entirely new role. The young girls will be sorry for me, sympathize with me, sigh for me; I chime in in just the same key; this is also a way of taking captive.

It's rather strange; I notice at this juncture with dismay that I am getting the symptom that Horace wished on every faithless girl – a black tooth, a front tooth at that. How superstitious we can be! The tooth really disturbs me, I find it quite hard to stand any allusion to it; it's a weak side I have. While otherwise I am fully armed, here even the biggest bungler can administer me a blow that goes far deeper than he thinks when he touches on the tooth. I do everything to make it white, but in vain. I say with Palnatoke:

> I rub it day and night,
> But I do not erase this dark shadow.

Life contains, after all, extraordinarily much puzzlement. A little thing like that can upset me more than the most dangerous assault, the most embarrassing situation. I want it extracted, yet that would interfere with my speaking voice and its power. But I want it out anyway, I want a false one put in; false to the world, that is; it was the black one that was false to me.

It's quite excellent that Cordelia finds an engagement an impediment. Marriage is and remains, after all, an honourable institution, even though it has the boring feature that from its very youth it receives part of the veneration brought by age. But an engagement, on the other hand, is a genuinely human invention, and so important and ridiculous on that account that it is quite all right for a young girl in the whirl of passion to place herself above it on the one hand, yet on the other to feel its importance, to feel her soul's energy, like a higher circulatory system, present everywhere within her. What is needed now is to steer her in such a way that in her bold flight she loses sight of marriage and of the mainland of reality in general, so that her soul, as much in its pride as in its anxiety about losing me, destroys an imperfect human form in order to hasten on to something higher than the ordinarily human. In this respect, however, I need have no fear, for her passage through life is already so floating and light that reality has already to a large extent been lost sight of. Besides, I am constantly on board and can always unfurl the sails.

Woman is and remains, after all, an inexhaustible topic for my reflections, an eternal profusion for my observations. Let the person who feels no urge for this study be whatever he likes in the world; one thing he is not: he is not an aesthetician. The glory and divinity of aesthetics is just this, that it only enters into relation with the beautiful, all it has to do with, essentially, is fiction and the fair sex. It can gladden me and my heart to imagine the sun of feminine loveliness radiating in an infinite diversity, spreading itself in a confusion of tongues where each individual has a small part of femininity's total wealth, yet so that what else she has forms itself harmoniously about that point. In this sense feminine beauty is infinitely divisible. Except that the particular share of beauty must be harmoniously controlled, for otherwise its effect will be disturbing and it will seem as though Nature's intentions for this woman had not been realized. My eyes can never weary of coursing over this multifaceted surface, these diffused emanations of womanly beauty. Every individual feature has its own small part and is yet complete, happy, glad, beautiful. Each has its own: the merry smile, the roguish glance, the longing eye, the pensive head, the exuberant spirits, the quiet sadness, the deep foreboding, the portending melancholy, the earthly homesickness, the unconfessed emotions, the beckoning brows, the questioning lips, the secretive forehead, the inveigling curls, the concealing lashes, the heavenly pride, the earthly modesty, the angelic purity, the secret blush, the graceful step, the lovely swaying, the languishing posture, the wistful dreaming, the unaccountable sighs, the willowy form, the soft outlines, the luxuriant bosom, the swelling hips, the tiny foot, the dainty hand. – Each has its own, what it has the other does not. When I have looked and looked again at, considered and considered again, this worldly multiplicity, when I have smiled, sighed, flattered, threatened, desired, tempted, laughed, wept, hoped, feared, won, lost – I close the fan and the scattered fragments gather themselves into the unity, the parts into the whole. My soul then rejoices, my heart pounds, my passion is inflamed. This one girl, the only one in all the world, she must belong to me, she must be mine. God can keep His heaven so long as I can keep her. I know what I'm choosing – something so great that it can't be to heaven's advantage to apportion things thus, for, if I kept her, what would be left over for heaven? The Muhammadan faithful would be disappointed in their hope were they, in their paradise, to embrace pale, weak shadows; for warm hearts they would not find, since all the warmth of the heart would be concentrated in her breast. Disconsolate, they would despair when they found pale lips, lacklustre eyes, an impassive bosom, a limp handclasp; for all the redness of the lips and the fire of the eyes and the heaving of the bosom and the promise of the handclasp and the foreboding of the sigh and the seal of the kiss and the trembling of the touch and the passion of the embrace – all – all would be united in her who lavished upon me a wealth sufficient for a whole world, both here and in the beyond. That's how I have often thought of this matter. But every time I think in this way I become warm, because I imagine her as warm. Although warmth is usually considered a good sign, it does not follow that this way of thinking will be accorded the distinction of being called 'solid'. So now, for the sake of variety, being myself cold I shall think coldly of woman. I shall try to think of woman categorially. Under what category must she be understood? Under being-for-another. This is not, however, to be taken in the bad sense, as if the one that was for me were also for another. Here, as always with abstract thought, one must refrain from having any regard to experience; for otherwise, in the present case, I would find, most curiously, that experience is both for and against me. Here as always, experience is a most curious character, because it is its nature always to be both for and against. So she is being-for-another. Here again, but from another quarter, one must not be put off by experience, which teaches us that one seldom encounters a woman who is truly being-for-another, since a great many are generally speaking absolutely nothing, either for themselves or for others. She shares this description with Nature, with anything feminine at all. Thus Nature as a whole is only for-another; not in the teleological sense in which the separate links in Nature exist for some other particular link, but in the sense that all of Nature is for-another – for Spirit. Similarly with particular things. Plant-life, for instance, unfolds its hidden charms in all naivety and is only for-another. Likewise a puzzle, a charade, a secret, a vowel, etc. are only for-another. And this can explain why, when God created Eve, He let a deep sleep fall upon Adam; for woman is the man's dream. There is also another way in which this story teaches that woman is being-for-another. For it is said that Jehovah took a rib from the man's side. Had he taken something, say, from the man's brain, woman would no doubt have remained a being-for-another; the idea, however, would not have been to make her a figment of the brain but something quite different. She became flesh and blood, but for that very reason she falls under the description 'Nature', which is essentially being-for-another. It is at the touch of love that she first awakens; before that she is dream. Yet we can distinguish two stages in that dream existence: the first is when love dreams about her, the second when she dreams about love.

As being-for-another, woman is characterized by pure virginity. For virginity is a form of being which, in so far as it is a being-for-self, is really an abstraction and it only appears for another. The same is true of feminine innocence. So one can say that a woman in that state is invisible. And we know there was no image of Vesta, the goddess who most nearly represented authentic virginity. For the form of this existence is aesthetic jealousy of oneself, just as Jehovah is ethically jealous of himself, and it will not allow there to be any image of it or even any notion. It is this contradiction, that what is for-another *is* not, and only becomes visible as it were with the other. Logically, there is nothing wrong with this contradiction, and no one who knows how to think logically will be put off by it but rejoice in it. Anyone who thinks illogically, however, will fancy that whatever has being-for-another simply *is*, in the finite sense in which one can say of a particular thing, 'That's something for me.'

This being of woman (for the word 'existence' already says too much, since she does not subsist out of herself) is rightly characterized as charm, an expression suggesting vegetative life; she is like a flower, as the poets are fond of saying, and even the spiritual is present in her in a vegetative manner. She is wholly contained in categories of Nature, and so she is free only aesthetically. She only becomes free in a deeper sense through the man, and that is why we say [in Danish] *at frie*, and that is why the man 'frees' [*frier*]. Certainly the woman chooses, but if we are thinking of this as the outcome of a long process of deliberation, the choice is unfeminine. That's why it is a humiliation to get a refusal, because the individual in question has thought too well of himself, has wanted to make another free without being able to. – There is a deep irony in this situation. The for-another has the appearance of being the dominant party: the man sues for her, the woman chooses. In terms of her concept a woman is the vanquished one; in terms of the man's he is the victor; and yet this victor bows before the vanquished. Still, that's quite natural and it is only boorishness, stupidity and lack of erotic sensibility to ignore what is immediately presented in this way. There is also a deeper reason. For the woman is substance, the man is reflection. So she doesn't choose, then, without further ado. The man sues, she chooses. But the suing is a question and her choice is just an answer to a question.

In one sense the man is more than the woman, in another he is infinitely less.

This being-for-another is pure virginity. If it makes an attempt to be itself in relation to another being which is being-for-it, then the opposition manifests itself in an absolute prudishness; but this opposition, too, shows that woman's essential being is being-for-another. Absolute devotion has as its diametrical opposite absolute prudishness, which is invisible in a converse sense as the abstraction against which everything breaks, but without this bringing the abstraction to life. Femininity then takes on the character of abstract cruelty, an extreme in caricature of authentic feminine refractoriness. A man can never be as cruel as a woman. Consult mythology, fable and folk-tales and you will find this corroborated. If one has to describe a principle of Nature whose mercilessness knows no bounds, then it is a virginal being. Or one reads in horror of a young woman who, unmoved, lets her suitors lay down their lives, something one finds so often in the folk-tales of all nations. A Bluebeard kills all the girls he has loved on the bridal night; but it is not the killing of them that he takes pleasure in; on the contrary, his pleasure has gone before. That is where the concreteness lies; it isn't cruelty for cruelty's sake. A Don Juan seduces them and runs away, but it is seducing them he takes pleasure in, not running away; so it is not at all this abstract cruelty.

Thus I see, the more I reflect on this matter, that my practice is in perfect harmony with my theory. For my practice has always been permeated with the conviction that woman is essentially being-for-another. That is why the moment is of infinite importance here; for being-for-another is always a matter of the moment. The moment may take a longer or a shorter time coming, but as soon as it comes, what was originally being-for-another becomes a relative being, and then it is all over. I am well aware that husbands, in another sense, say something to the effect that the woman is being-for-another, that she is everything to them for the whole of their lives. Of course one must give the husbands credit for that. But really I believe it is something they delude one another into thinking. Every class in society has, as a rule, certain conventional practices, and in particular certain conventional lies. This sailor's yarn must be reckoned among them. To be a judge of the moment is not such an easy matter, and naturally what a person who misjudges it lands himself in for the whole of his life is simply tedium. The moment is everything, and in the moment the woman is everything. The consequences I do not comprehend. Among them is the consequence of having children. Now I fancy that I am a fairly consistent thinker, but even if I were to go crazy I am not a man to consider this consequence; I simply do not understand it; you need a husband for that.

Yesterday Cordelia and I visited a family at their summer home. The party kept mostly to the garden, where we passed away the time in all sorts of physical exercise. Among other things we played quoits. When another gentleman who had been playing with Cordelia had gone, I took the opportunity to take his place. What a wealth of charm she displayed, even more seductive through the becoming exertion of the game! What graceful harmony in the contradictions of her movements! How light she was – like a dance over the meadows! How vigorous, yet unopposed, deceiving the eye until equilibrium resolved everything. How vehement her appearance, how challenging her glance! The game itself naturally held a special interest for me. Cordelia seemed not to notice it. A remark of mine to one of the spectators about the attractive custom of exchanging rings struck down in her soul like a lightning bolt. From that moment a higher radiance pervaded the whole situation, a deeper significance permeated it, a greater energy kindled her. I held both rings on my stick. I paused a moment. I exchanged a few words with the bystanders. She understood this pause. I tossed the rings to her again. Soon she caught both of them on her stick. As though inadvertently, she tossed them straight up into the air, so that it was impossible for me to catch them. This toss was accompanied by a look full of boundless temerity. There's a story of how a French soldier who had campaigned in Russia had his leg amputated at the knee because of gangrene. As soon as the painful operation was over, he grabbed the leg by the foot, threw it in the air and shouted: '*Vive l'empereur!*' With the same kind of look, and more beautiful than ever, she threw both rings into the air and said to herself: Long live love! I found it inadvisable, however, to let her run riot in this mood, or to leave her alone in it, for fear of the languor that so often ensues. I therefore remained quite calm and compelled her with the help of the presence of those around us to continue playing, as if I had noticed nothing. Conduct of that kind simply gives her more resilience.

If one could expect any sympathy these days for such inquiries, I would pose the prize question: 'Aesthetically, who is the more bashful, a young girl or a young matron, the ignorant or the knowledgeable? To which of them dare one grant greater freedom?' But such things don't concern these earnest times of ours. In Greece such an inquiry would have aroused general interest; the whole state would have been in commotion, the young girls and young wives in particular. No one would believe it nowadays, but nor would they believe it nowadays if they were told of the famous contest waged between two Greek girls and the extremely thorough inquiry it led to. For in Greece one did not treat these things lightly and irresponsibly. Yet everyone knows that Venus bears a nickname as a result of this contest, and that all admire the image of Venus which has immortalized her. A married woman has two periods in her life when she is interesting: her earliest youth and then again, long after, when she has become a great deal older. But she has also – this must not be denied her – a moment when she is even more charming than a young girl, and inspires even more respect; but it is a rare moment in life which need not be seen in life itself, and perhaps never is so. I imagine her, then, healthy, blooming, luxuriantly developed; she holds a child in her arms, on whom all her attention is turned, in whose contemplation she is lost. It is a picture one might call the most charming human life has to offer; it is a Nature myth, which may therefore only be seen in art, not in reality. Nor must there be any additional figures in the picture, no setting, for that would only disturb. If one has resort to our churches one has frequent opportunity to see a mother approaching with a child in her arms. Quite apart from the disconcerting wail of the child, and the anxious thoughts the wailing arouses about the parents' expectations for the child's future, the surroundings are in themselves so confusing that, even if everything else were perfect, the effect would be lost. One sees the father, and that is a great mistake since it removes the myth, the enchantment; one sees – *horrendo refero* – the earnest choir of godparents, and one sees – simply nothing. Conceived as a picture for the imagination it is the most charming thing of all. I am not without courage and daring, nor recklessness enough to venture an assault – but if I saw such an image in reality, I would be defenceless.

How Cordelia occupies me! Yet the time is soon over, for my soul constantly requires rejuvenation. It is already as though I heard the cock crowing in the distance. Perhaps she hears it too, but she believes it proclaims dawn. – Oh why is a young girl so pretty, and why does it last so briefly? I could become quite melancholy with this thought, and yet it is no concern of mine. Enjoy, don't chatter. Those who make a business of such reflections generally have no enjoyment at all. However, letting the thought of it come out can do no harm; for generally this sadness, not on one's own but on others' behalf, adds a little to one's male beauty. A sadness which dawns deceptively, like a misty veil, over manly strength is part of the masculine erotic. In the woman the corresponding quality is a kind of melancholy. – When a girl first gives herself totally it is all over. I still approach a young girl with a certain anxiety; my heart throbs because I feel the eternal power latent in her nature. That has never struck me in the presence of a married woman. The modicum of resistance she tries, with artful means, to put up is nothing. It's as if the married woman's cap should make a greater impression than a young girl's uncovered head. That is why Diana has always been my ideal. That pure virginity, that absolute decorousness, has always greatly engaged me. But while indeed occupied by her, I have always looked at her askance. For I take it she really in no way deserved all the praise she reaped for her virginity. She knew the role it played in her life; that is why she preserved it. Also, I have heard mumblings in philological corners that she retained an image of the terrible birth pangs her mother had endured. This is said to have put her off and I can't blame Diana for that, for I say with Euripides: I would rather go to war three times than bear one child. Now I couldn't really fall in love with Diana, but I don't deny I'd give a lot for a conversation with her, for what I might call a straight talk. She had to get used to all sorts of tricks. Obviously my good Diana possesses, in one way or another, a knowledge that makes her far less naive even than Venus. I wouldn't bother spying on her in her bath, not at all, but I'd like to spy her out with my questions. If I were stealing off to a tryst where I feared for my victory, I would prepare myself, arm myself, mobilize all the spirits of love, by conversing with her. –

It has often been a matter of consideration for me what situation, what moment, might be regarded as the most seductive. The answer to this naturally depends on what one desires and how one desires and the way one has developed. I go for the wedding-day and for one moment in particular. When she stands decked out as a bride yet all her magnificence pales before her beauty, and she too turns pale, when the blood stops, when her bosom rests, when the look falters, when the foot is unsteady, when the virgin trembles, when the fruit ripens; when heaven exalts her, when the seriousness gives her strength, when the promise sustains her, when the prayer blesses her, when the myrtle wreath crowns her; when the heart trembles, when the eyes are fixed on the ground, when she hides in herself, when she belongs other than to the world in order wholly to belong to it; when her bosom swells, when the living form sighs, when the voice falters, when the tear quivers before the riddle is explained, when the torch is lighted, when the bridegroom waits – then the moment has come. Soon it will be too late. There is only one step left but it is all that a false step needs. This moment makes even an insignificant girl significant, even a little Zerlina becomes a subject. Everything must be composed, the biggest contrasts united in the moment; if something is missing, especially one of the chief contrasts, the situation immediately loses part of its seductiveness. There is a well-known engraving. It represents a penitent. She looks so young and innocent that one is almost embarrassed on her and her confessor's behalf about what she can really have to confess. She is lifting her veil a little, she is looking out into the world as if seeking something she might on some later occasion have an opportunity to confess, and of course one understands that indeed it is nothing more than obligation out of consideration to – the father-confessor. The situation is really most seductive, and since she is the only figure in the piece, there is nothing to prevent one's imagining the church in which all this takes place being so spacious that several very different preachers could all preach here simultaneously. Yes, the situation is really most seductive, and I have no objection to being placed in the background, especially if the girl has nothing against it. However, it will always be an extremely subordinate situation; after all, it appears that it is not only in her relation to a father-confessor that the girl is a child, and it will take time before the moment comes.

Now have I, in my relationship with Cordelia, been constantly faithful to my pact? That is to say, to my pact with the aesthetic. For that is what makes me strong, the fact that I always have the idea on my side. It is a secret, like Samson's hair, which no Delilah shall wrest from me. Straightforwardly to betray a young girl, that is something I certainly couldn't endure. But the fact that the idea, too, is there in motion, that it is in its service that I act and to its service that I dedicate myself, that makes me strict with myself, an abstainer from every forbidden enjoyment. Has the interesting always been preserved? Yes, in this secret conversation I dare say it freely and openly. The engagement itself was interesting precisely in not offering what is ordinarily understood by the interesting. It preserved the interesting through the outward appearance contradicting the inner life. Had I been secretly bound to her, it would only have been interesting to the first power. This, however, is interesting to the second power, and for that reason interesting for the first time for her. The betrothal bursts, but by virtue of the fact that she herself cancels it in order to raise herself to a higher sphere. So it should be; for this is the form of the interesting which will occupy her most.

September 16th

The bond burst; longingly, strong, daring, divine, she flies like a bird which is allowed now for the first time to stretch its wings. Fly, bird, fly! Truly, if this royal flight were a departure from me, my pain would be infinitely deep. As if Pygmalion's beloved were turned to stone again, that is how it would be for me. I have made her light, light as a thought; shouldn't this, my thought, belong to me? It would be something to despair over. A moment earlier it would not have occupied me, a moment later it will not trouble me, but now – now – this now which is an eternity to me. But she does not fly away from me. Fly, then, bird, fly; rise proudly on your wings, glide through the soft realms of the air, soon I am with you, soon I will be hiding myself with you in that deep solitude!

The aunt was somewhat taken aback by the news. However, she is too much the free-thinker to want to coerce Cordelia, even though, partly to lull her into an even sounder sleep, partly to confuse Cordelia a little, I have made some attempts at getting her to take an interest on my behalf. As for that, she otherwise shows me much sympathy; she has no notion of what good reason I have to deprecate all sympathy.

She has got permission from the aunt to spend some time in the country; she is to visit a family. It is very fortunate that she cannot straightaway surrender to an excess of mood. It means she will be kept in a state of tension for a while yet by all kinds of outside resistance. I keep up a tenuous communication with her with the help of letters; that keeps our relationship alive. She must be made strong now in every way; in particular the best will be to let her have a few flings at eccentric contempt for people and the commonplace. Then when the day of departure arrives, a dependable fellow will turn up as her coachman. They will be joined outside the gate by my highly trusted servant. He accompanies them to the appointed place and remains with her for her service and assistance in case of need. Next to myself I know of no one better fitted for this than Johan. I have myself arranged everything out there as tastefully as possible. Nothing lacks that can serve in any way to beguile her soul and reassure it with a sense of luxurious wellbeing.

My Cordelia!

So far the separate family cries of 'Fire!' have not joined in a general capitoline city-war's confusion. Presumably you have already had to put up with individual solos. Imagine the whole assembly of tea-and-rum and coffee mesdames; imagine a lady presiding who forms a worthy counterpart to Claudius's immortal President Lars, and you have a picture, a conception, and a measure of what you have lost and with whom: being well thought of by good people.

I enclose the famous engraving which represents President Lars. I couldn't purchase it separately, so I bought the whole of Claudius, tore it out and threw away the rest, for how could I venture to trouble you with a gift that at this moment has no meaning for you? Why shouldn't I use every means to get hold of what might give you pleasure just for one moment? Why should I let more get mixed up in a situation that belongs to it? Nature may be given to such excesses, and the person who is in thrall to all of life's finite circumstances. But you, my Cordelia, in your freedom you would hate it.

Your Johannes

Spring is the most beautiful time to fall in love, autumn the most beautiful to reach the goal of one's desires. In the autumn lies a sadness which is entirely in keeping with the way the thought of a desire's fulfilment courses through one. Today I have been out at the country place where in a few days Cordelia will find a setting in harmony with her soul. I myself do not want to share in her surprise and pleasure over this; such erotic issues would only weaken her soul. If she is alone in this, on the other hand, she will pass her time in reverie over such things. Everywhere she will see allusions, hints, an enchanted world, but all of this would lose its meaning if I stood by her side; it would make her forget that, for us, the time is past when such things enjoyed in fellowship had meaning. The surroundings must not inveigle her soul like a narcotic, but constantly allow it to rise up out of them by looking upon them as a game of no significance compared with what is to come. I intend in these days that remain to visit this place more often to keep me in the mood.

My Cordelia!

I can now truly call you *mine*, no outward sign reminds me of my possession. – Soon I shall truly call you *mine*. And when I hold you firmly in my arms, when you entwine me in your embrace, we need no ring to remind us that we belong to each other, for is not this embrace a ring that is more than a symbol? And the more firmly this ring closes round us, the more inseparably it unites us, the more freedom, for your freedom consists in being mine, as mine in being yours.

Your Johannes

My Cordelia!

While out hunting, Alpheus fell in love with the nymph Arethusa. She would not grant his prayer but fled constantly before him, until on the island of Ortygia she was changed into a fountain. So bitterly did Alpheus sorrow over this that he was changed into a river in Elis on the Peloponnese. He did not forget his love, however, but united himself beneath the sea with that fountain. Is the time of metamorphosis past? Answer: Is the time of love past? With what should I compare your pure deep soul, which has no ties with the world, except with a fountain? And have I not said to you that I am like a river that has fallen in love? And do I not plunge now beneath the sea, now we are separated, to be united with you? There under the sea we meet again, for it is in these depths that we really belong together.

Your Johannes

My Cordelia!

Soon, soon you are mine. When the sun closes its searching eye, when history is over and the myths begin, then it is not only my cloak I fling about me, I fling the night about me just like a cloak and hasten to you and hearken to find you, not by footfalls but by the beating of your heart.

Your Johannes

These days, when I cannot be with her in person whenever I want, the thought has troubled me that it might occur to her at some moment to consider the future. So far that hasn't happened; I have been too good at drugging her aesthetically. Nothing less erotic is imaginable than this talk of the future, the reason for which is basically that people have nothing with which to fill the present. When I'm there I have no fear of that either, for I can make her forget both time and eternity. If one doesn't know how to put oneself in rapport with a girl, one should never get involved in trying to beguile, for then it will be impossible to avoid the two reefs: questions about the future and a catechism on faith. Thus it is quite right of Gretchen to hold a little examination of this kind for Faust, since he had taken the imprudent step of playing the knight, and against an assault of that kind a girl is always armed.

Now everything is, I think, in order for her reception; she must not want of opportunity to admire my powers of memory, or rather, she must not have time to admire it. Nothing has been overlooked which might have some significance for her, while on the other hand, there is nothing there that could directly remind her of me, while invisibly I am nevertheless present everywhere. But the effect will largely depend on how she comes to see it for the first time. Here my servant has received the most detailed instructions, and he is in his way a complete virtuoso. He knows how to drop remarks carelessly to order; he knows how to be ignorant, in short he is invaluable to me. – The location is as she could wish. If one sits in the middle of the room, in both directions one has a view beyond anything in the foreground, on both sides one has the endless horizon, one is alone in the wide ocean of the atmosphere. If one approaches a row of windows on the one side, there far on the horizon a forest curves in on itself like a wreath, delimiting and enclosing. That's how it should be. What does love love? – an enclosure; wasn't Paradise itself an enclosed place, a garden towards the east? – But this ring closes itself too tightly about one – one comes nearer the window, a calm lake hides humbly amidst the higher ground encircling it. At its edge lies a boat. A sigh from the fullness of the heart, a breath from thought's unrest – it frees itself from its moorings, it glides over the surface of the lake, softly moved by the gentle breezes of inexpressible longing; one disappears into the secretive solitude of the forest, cradled by the surface of the lake, which dreams of the forest's dark depths. One turns to the other side, where the open sea spreads before the unhindered eye, pursued by thoughts with nothing to detain them. – What does love love? Infinitude. – What does love fear? Limitation. – Behind this large salon is a smaller room, or rather a closet; for whatever that room in the Wahl house was on the verge of being, this is it. The similarity is striking. A carpet woven of osiers covers the floor; before the sofa stands a small tea-table, on it a lamp, the image of the one at home. Everything is the same, only more splendid. It's a difference I feel I can permit myself with the room. In the salon stands a piano, a very plain one, but reminiscent of the fortepiano at the Jansens'. It is open; on the music stand a little Swedish melody lies open. The door into the entry stands ajar. She comes in by the door at the back of the room – Johan has been instructed in this. Her eye then takes in the closet and the piano together. Memory awakens in her soul; just then Johan opens the door. – The illusion is perfect. She goes into the closet. She is pleased, of that I'm sure. As her glance falls on the table she sees a book. The same instant Johan picks it up as if to lay it to one side, as he adds casually, 'The master must have forgotten this when he was out here this morning.' From that she first learns that already this morning I have been out there, and then she wants to see the book. It is a German translation of Apuleius's well-known *Cupid and Psyche*. It is no poetic work, but nor should it be; for it is always an insult to a young girl to offer her a piece of genuine poetry, as if she herself were not poetical enough in such moments to absorb the poetry hidden in them before it is consumed by another's thought. This is not something people generally consider, and yet it is so. – She will read this book and thus the purpose is achieved. – In opening it at the place where it was last read she will find a little sprig of myrtle; she will also find that it means rather more than a bookmarker.

My Cordelia!

What fear? When we keep together we are strong, stronger than the world, stronger than the gods themselves. You know, there once lived a race on earth who, though human, were each sufficient unto themselves and did not know the inner union of love. Yet they were mighty, so mighty that they would storm heaven. Jupiter feared them and divided them up so that one became two, a man and a woman. Now it happens sometimes that what was earlier united is brought together once more in love; such a union is stronger than Jupiter. Then they are not merely as strong as was the individual but even stronger, for love's union is an even higher one.

Your Johannes

September 24th

The night is still – the clock strikes a quarter to twelve. – The keeper by the gate blows his benediction out over the countryside. It echoes back from Blegdammen – he goes inside the gate – he blows again, it echoes even further. – Everything sleeps in peace, except love. So rise up, you secret powers of love, unite in this breast! The night is silent – a solitary bird breaks this silence with its screech and the beat of its wings as it skims over the dewy field down the sloping bank to its rendezvous – *accipio omen*! How full of omens all Nature is! I take warning from the flight of the birds, from their cries, from the playful slap of the fish against the water's surface, from their disappearance beneath the depths, from a distant barking of dogs, from a wagon's faraway clatter, from footfalls that echo from afar. No ghosts do I see in this night hour; I do not see what has been, but what shall be, from the bosom of the lake, from the kiss of the dew, from the mist that spreads over the earth and hides its fruitful embrace. Everything is image; I myself am a myth about myself, for is it not rather as a myth that I hasten to this meeting? Who I am has nothing to do with it. Everything finite and temporal is forgotten, only the eternal remains, the power of love, its longing, its bliss. – My soul is attuned as a drawn bow, my thoughts ready as arrows in a quiver, not poisoned yet well able to mingle with blood. How vigorous is my soul, healthy, happy, all-present like a god. – Her beauty came from Nature. I thank you, wonderful Nature! Like a mother you have watched over her. Accept my thanks for your care. She was undefiled. I thank you, you people to whom she owed that. Her development was my handiwork – soon I shall enjoy my reward. – How much have I gathered into this one moment which is now at hand. Death and damnation if I should fail! –

I don't see my carriage yet. – I hear the crack of a whip, it's my coachman. – Drive for dear life, even if the horses drop dead, but not one second before we are there.

September 25th

Why can't a night like that be longer? If Alectryon could put a foot wrong, why can't the sun be compassionate enough to do the same? Still, now it is over and I want never to see her again. Once a girl has given away everything, she is weak, she has lost everything; for in the man innocence is a negative factor, while for the woman it is her whole worth. Now all resistance is impossible, and only when it is there is it beautiful to love; once it is gone, love is only weakness and habit. I do not wish to be reminded of my relation to her; she has lost her fragrance, and the time has gone when, for pain over her untrue lover, a girl is transformed into a heliotrope. I will not take leave of her; nothing disgusts me more than a woman's tears and a woman's prayers, which change everything yet are really of no consequence. I have loved her, but from now on she can no longer engage my soul. If I were a god I would do for her what Neptune did for a nymph: change her into a man.

Nevertheless, it would really be worthwhile knowing whether one couldn't poetize oneself out of a girl, whether one couldn't make her so proud that she imagined it was she who had wearied of the relationship. It could become a quite interesting epilogue, which in its own right might be of psychological interest, and besides that, enrich one with many erotic observations.